CU00809917

The Dragon Keeper

Abby Woodland

Published by Abby Woodland, 2023.

THE DRAGON KEEPER

First edition. September 15, 2023.

Copyright © 2023 Abby Woodland.

ISBN: 979-8223599944

Written by Abby Woodland.

Table of Contents

To those who believed in me when I never did. Thank you.

The Escape

The night was blistery and dense as a tall, hooded figure glided across the rain-soaked grass. She lifted her head to the sky. Nothing but storm clouds and darkness. Not even the moon could shine through the thick clouds. She removed her hood, letting the rain caress her skin as she waited for him... for the only person she knew that could save her. The trees blew in the breeze, rustling gently and growing in cadence as the wind pushed against them harder. An old man came stumbling through the forest carrying a staff with a ball made of clear stone perched on top. The woman ran up to him.

"He's after me. He knows I left!" She whispered in a panic, clutching the old man, holding him upright as another gust of wind came, nearly knocking the man over.

He put his hands on her shoulders, partially to steady himself, partially for reassurance. "I know. But do not worry, Andromeda. We *will* hide you. It will take some time and a great deal of magic on your end. Can you manage it?"

"Yes, *please* Wilbur. I'll do whatever it takes." She shivered from both cold and fear. The risk of weakening her powers was worth the escape.

"Then come with me. We'll disguise you as my niece. They won't likely search for you there unless they sense the connection between our pasts. I have done my best to erase it though." Wilbur gripped his walking stick tighter and looked over Andromeda's shoulder. "You need to disguise yourself now. Do not let them recognize you. The change you pick may become permanent, so make sure it is a figure you can live with. You will have to wear it always. Come. We need to move fast before they get here." He grasped her arm and led her through the forest, into a deep thicket of trees just as the dark, smoking figures of black horses appeared.

"Night Mares!" Andromeda whispered. Wilbur hushed her and shoved her forward, deeper into the woods. Andromeda looked back, eyes wide with fear.

"Stay quiet. We must get to the village gates before they do. They are swift. We can't outrun them, and they might pick up on your scent soon. Disguise yourself now. Hurry!" He stepped back as she muttered some words under her breath. Her blonde hair changed a deep, chestnut brown and her skin, slightly tanned to that of a farm girl's. Her height shrank by two inches, and she plumped her face slightly, changing her clothing to brown and green to complement her now blueish green eyes, no longer gray as most sorceresses' eyes were. Her transformation was complete.

"Call me Felicity." She said to Wilbur.

"My niece Felicity," He replied. "Come, we must hasten!" They raced through the trees to the edge of the forest where the gate to Imyr stood, branches and bushes scratching and tugging at them with every turn. Getting to the large, stone gate was their only hope for protection now. Wilbur shoved

Andromeda, now Felicity, through the w
whinny of the Night Mares, closing in be
called out to the gateman, who climbed off h.
them.

"Who are you and what is your business .
asked.

"It is I, Wilbur, Solengrad. I must come in. I haa
my niece through the woods. She is easily lost. She is co.
live with me at my farm." He was panting now, desperate to
in.

"Ah yes, and your name dear?" He asked, looking a
Andromeda.

"Andro...um... I am Felicity." She replied, pretending to be
shy, but really trying to control her breathing after rushing to
the gate. She almost blew her cover.

"A beautiful name for a very pretty girl. Come in you two,
out of the storm now." Solengrad opened the gate door and let
them in, "You travel very light my dear." The gateman said, as
the gate door creaked open. He was eyeing her suspiciously.

"Indeed, she does. Her family died in a fire and their farm
burned down. Now I care for her. I needed help at my place."
The old men eyed each other, with Solengrad, looking at his
friend with curiosity. Wilbur knew he suspected his lies but
was not one to pry more than that. Women travelers were rare
in Imyr and when they did come, it was on horseback.

"Well come on then. Don't just stand there. Get inside,
warm her up. Don't need her dying of pneumonia before the
men in this town get a look at her." He replied with a chuckle,
shutting the door behind them as the Night Mares rode up.

Thank you, friend." Wilbur replied. They walked away the gate, hastening through the town to the fields at the end. "Move fast but don't run. We can't attract attention." Wilbur whispered to Felicity. She nodded, lifting the hem of her skit that had mud caked on it up to her knees. By the time they arrived at the farm, they were dirty, scratched up, and exhausted, though the adrenaline kept them going this far. They were silent as the storm picked up and it was too loud for them to hear each other, let alone have the breath to speak. Wilbur threw open the wooden door to his farmhouse. They set their things down as he started a fire, then he turned to Felicity and spoke.

"I am sorry to say that Solengrad is very inappropriate sometimes. Don't pay him any mind. He doesn't always say rude things." Wilbur told her as a clap of thunder shook the tiny house. Wilbur grabbed a kettle of water, placed it on a hook over the fire, and sat in the chair next to Felicity.

"It's ok. I'm not too worried about it. It's a fair exchange for safety tonight." Felicity replied.

"A good point. Come, let me show you your room. It's small. It was once my daughter's and then your mother's when she stayed with me." He indicated to a ladder next to the fireplace that led to a loft. Wilbur's bed was tucked behind the ladder on the main floor next to the fire.

"Thank you again. So very much." Felicity replied.

"Anything for family." Wilbur chuckled at that statement.

"Dear Uncle, with your sense of humor." She chuckled, now feeling the fear in her subside. This was the new normal now. She would have to hold up this ruse for the rest of her life. She would need to stay hidden where her mother was once hidden.

Sadness overwhelmed her as a tear slid down her face. She took a stone out of her bag and stared at it. Was this thing worth it? It shook a little. Outside, it was a beautiful, red stone, or so it seemed. Inside, no one knew it contained a dragon. Felicity gave it a hug. It was safe for now. It was, as far as she knew, the only dragon egg that was left in Domandunn, where she had escaped from. Now, Tristan and his father had no dragons. She had to keep it that way. Her heart sank thinking about the man she loved. *Tristan.* She cried harder, wiping her tears on a handkerchief from her dress pocked. She hugged the dragon egg again. "You'll be safe now, little one." She whispered.

Felicity

It had been a close call...again. The Mage Prince sent his soldiers out to keep looking for Felicity and the dragon's egg. One of his scouts had seen her the night Wilbur saved her. She had just passed beyond the gates. Felicity had to leave and find another safe place to stay. She couldn't risk putting anyone else in danger. Besides, she had her disguise and that should be enough to keep her hidden, right? But Wilbur refused to let her go. He said it would look suspicious if she left just as she arrived, and that she would be safer with walls around her and the egg than she would in the woods away from protection. So, she stayed. Not because she believed in what Wilbur was saying, though maybe to an extent she did, but because she knew that the egg needed to be protected. Her mother had tried to save all the eggs, but it had led to destruction. Now, it was her turn and she NEEDED to be successful this time around.

Felicity went out into the barn. She tossed her dark hair over her shoulder, not realizing she was being watched. She walked up to one of the horses, a chestnut brown mare that was with child and due any day now. She bent down low and checked her belly and rear. She was starting to dilate but wasn't quite ready for delivery yet. Felicity put fresh straw into the stall and brought her some water. The mare was restless, and it was almost time to call Wilbur in from the fields to help her deliver the horse. She had never done this before but was feeling excited.

Where Felicity was from, their mares were made of smoke and fire because of their magic. It was rare to find a horse with blood and bone. Here, they were just regular horses, the ones their Night Mares were made to copy. The Mage King wouldn't allow them to have mortal animals. He saw them as weak and not fit for battle. Everything was about war with him. And it wasn't that Felicity hadn't seen real animals before, but she had never been in charge of them. Her gift of being able to heal and care for animals had to be kept a secret. She had to hide her powers even when she thought she was safe. Her mother told her that because of the gift they had over magical *and* mortal creatures, she would be hunted down and forced to help their King with his evil plan of weaponizing dragons, or worse, she would be killed if she denied him. Felicity was terrified at that thought. This made her more cautious, at least until Tristan.

At the time, she had fallen in love with the King's son. She was set to marry him that year. She felt safe enough with him to confide in him when it came to her powers. She had demonstrated to him, using a bird with a hurt wing. She healed the bird watching it fly off. Tristan betrayed her and told his father about her magic. He said that she was the one to hatch the dragons and heal them, so they'd never die. The King sent some men to collect her, and her mother died, fighting them off. Felicity escaped and made her way to Wilbur, who was now protecting her.

Felicity went back to tending to the mare and feeding the other animals. Wilbur told her he had a farm hand, but she had been there a month and hadn't seen him. Wilbur said that he had to care for his dying mother and younger siblings, but that he would be returning to the farm that day. She hoped that he knew how to deliver a foal because she wasn't prepared to do anything of the sort. Wilbur said he would help her if the farm hand didn't show, but once he started plowing, it was hard to get his attention and make him stop. Felicity started mucking out all the stalls and putting in fresh hay when the most beautiful man walked into the barn. Though she was still hurting, she had never seen someone so perfect in her life.

He smiled at her, taking her in. "Hello. You must be Felicity." The man replied. He couldn't have been older than twenty-four.

"Um, yes. I-I-I am." She stuttered, completely embarrassed by her reply. She noticed the smell of muck on her shoes and hoped the man wouldn't notice it too.

"Wonderful. Wilbur said you'd be here. I'm Thomas, but you can call me Tom for short. I'm the farm hand that Wilbur hired several summers ago. I am so sorry you've been stuck with the extra work. My mother had passed, and I had to care for our family for a short time. I hope it wasn't too much of an inconvenience for you." He gave her another smile that showed off his dimpled cheeks and perfect teeth. Felicity's heart stopped. He wasn't what she expected a farm hand to look like. Tom waited for her to respond.

Felicity took a breath and said, "Oh it was fine. I don't mind the hard work. Keeps me busy since I'm still new here."

"I'm glad you found some solace in it then. I can take over now though," he paused, "unless you wanted to stay and work together. Then I could come help you with other chores." He looked at her and smiled the most perfect smile she'd ever seen. Felicity could feel herself blush before busying herself with the mare.

Felicity noticed the mare was fully dilated and ready to push. She could see the muscles contracting in her chestnut belly. "Of course! That would be nice. This mare is ready to labor now anyways. I've never done this before. Are you skilled in this?" She felt awkward asking him to deliver a horse with her upon their first meeting, but it would save time getting Wilbur.

"Of course! I've raised Belle since she was a filly. I was the one who delivered her here and now I get to deliver her foal. I feel like today is going to be a day of luck." He smiled again at Felicity.

She was glad her 'uncle' had hired this man. He was kind and she needed someone to be kind to her right now.

"Could you fetch some clean towels? Wilbur has some in that wooden box over there, specifically for animal births." He pointed to a large, wooden crate in the corner of the barn. Felicity went and pulled out several large towels and sheets. She brought them over to Tom and he set them near the water, "Unlike a human baby, you don't have to keep them warm and covered up. But it helps to have these to clear the face off and if the heart drops on the foal, we will have to deliver quickly and keep them both warm. Luckily, it's fall, and the weather isn't quite as cold yet, so we don't have to worry about snow and temperature drops. But if it was winter, we would need these for both mom and baby." He was very knowledgeable about a lot of things. Felicity wondered why he wasn't a teacher instead of a farm hand.

"You know so much about these animals. Shouldn't you be a scholar instead of working with my uncle?" She blurted out without thinking.

"I should have but I couldn't. There wasn't enough money to send me to school. I read and write, and I can do math, but things like science and all the other amazing things you learn in the cities and other places just aren't in my future." Tom said it so matter-of-factly that Felicity felt sad for him. She wished she could make that happen for him one day. She wondered if Wilbur was trying to help him with it too.

Felicity sighed deeply. She felt sorry for him. "I hope one day you get to go." She whispered. She could see that he was ear to stomach with Belle now but couldn't stop looking at him. He had a sad but strong look on his face. She knew this was something he was used to hearing and it pained him.

Tom sat back up and looked at Felicity. "I do too, but now is not the time for it. I think Belle is ready to push!" He moved some of the hay around Belle and went from kneeling to crouching. "You're going to want to watch the foal's hooves. They sometimes kick when they come out." Felicity backed up a bit, looking at Tom sheepishly. He gave her a small smile and that made her feel more confident.

It was a long labor, and they were all exhausted, but in the end, Belle delivered a beautiful black and brown colt, that they named Jonas. They cleaned him up and got him to cuddle up next to Belle who was panting, exhausted from the extensive labor. Tom brought her some water and she drank it up. Jonas was strong and already trying to move around a lot. He wasn't nursing yet, but Tom said it took some time for the new colt to adjust.

"I should go tell my uncle he was born. He wanted a male." Felicity replied standing up and trying not to slip in the mess of birth. She didn't want to leave Tom, but she had to. The urge to kiss him in celebration over this new horse would be crossing the line and she didn't want to scare Tom off.

"Alright then. I will finish cleaning up here though you should probably clean yourself up a bit before going to the field. He might get startled seeing you covered in blood. You've a bit of horse mess on the hem of your dress and your sleeves too." Felicity flushed as she inspected herself. There was indeed some horse poo and lots of other unknown fluids that soaked her. She was sticky and hay was clinging to her. Felicity could feel her face hot with embarrassment.

"Right. Of course." She ran to the house to change and wash up, then back out to the field where Wilbur had just set down his plow to drink water from a bucket. He was thrilled when he heard the news. He dropped everything and raced back towards the barn to see the new colt.

"Did you name him?" He asked Felicity, panting. He wasn't as young as he used to be.

"Jonas." Felicity said.

"A fitting name for such a fine horse." He said. "I can't wait to see what he becomes." This hit Felicity differently. Wilbur was such a wonderful person. He always saw the good in others and was eager to help people and animals whenever possible. Felicity knew now why her mom wanted her to see him when she was in danger. He would protect her till his last breath. She could feel it.

Wilbur

The next few days were very busy. With Jonas to care for, house and farm chores to catch up on now that Tom was back and able to help, and now the town social coming up, Felicity had work to do from sunup to sundown. She would pitter patter around the house the way her mother used to. This made Wilbur chuckle.

On the other hand, now that Tom was back, Wilbur had less work and was more than happy to interfere with his charge and her life. He had secretly gone into town and bought Felicity a beautiful pink dress to compliment her disguised features. He was hoping that she would wear it to the town social and that she would go with Tom. He normally wouldn't have done that, but he could see the way that she was looking at Tom as they worked, and the way Tom was looking at her. He wasn't one for distractions, having married once and his only child passing during childbirth along with his wife, but it didn't mean that he couldn't give a little push to these two lovebirds if he wanted. He knew that Tom would be taken with her even more at the social if she showed up all dressed up and not covered in manure and other mashes of filth. And besides, who was he to get in the way of love between two young people in love?

Wilbur was not much of a romantic, but he was a troublemaker, and he did promise Andromeda's mom, no, Felicity's mom, that he was going to look after her and keep her safe if she should ever contact him. He had to for the fate of an entire race and possibly the world. Felicity didn't know much about his relationship with her mom. She didn't know that they were technically cousins. It was part of the reason he wanted her to call him uncle. He didn't want the true connection discovered, though this one would be close enough if Hadrion tried to discover them. She didn't know that he had magic like her too, but it had been lost after the first war for the dragon's safety. She didn't know much about the war either or why her mom was killed since she had only been a teen. Her mother kept her in the dark as much as she could. There was too much at stake and they had to protect her. Wilbur had been part of the reason her mom was killed. He wanted to keep that part a secret but was not sure how. He wanted to protect Felicity as her mom had, but he wondered how long he could keep up that ruse. He wasn't prepared to tell her that he was part of the reason she was an orphan. She had already lost her father before the war due to illness. She didn't need to lose him too. He didn't want her to have that sort of pain again.

Wilbur called Felicity after Tom went home. He wanted to make this a surprise. "Close your eyes and follow me, my dear." He told her, taking her hand and leading her to her room. He guided her up the steps slowly, hoping she wouldn't trip. "Open your eyes!" She opened them and gasped. On her bed was the pink dress. Soft and beautiful, it was the most glorious thing she had ever seen. It had lace around the collar, cuffs, and hem of the dress, with small pearls at the center of the lace flowers. He had also gotten her a pair of black boots and white petti coat. She had never been more pleased to see such beautiful things. Nor had she owned such a luxurious thing in her life.

"Um, so this is embarrassing, but you'll have to go to the dress shop for a corset fitting. I didn't want to ask, and I didn't know what size to get. It's not proper for an uncle to know those things." He gave her a small, embarrassed smile, blushing as he did so. "Emily will help you with that. She is the seamstress's daughter, and she runs the front end of the haberdashery. She can get things sorted out. She's your age so it shouldn't be as embarrassing for you as it was for me to set the appointment." Wilbur blushed and looked at the ground.

Felicity hugged him, "Thank you uncle. This is a wonderful gift and very much appreciated and needed. I haven't had much in the way of clothing to fit my new self." She winked at him and smiled. She had been wearing the same three sets of clothes daily, but using magic to make them change colors, or if she was washing them, to sew faster since she had to make clothes out of feed cloth for the time being. This time, she could have another thing to wear that wasn't scratchy and coarse. This was something beautiful.

"It's my pleasure. Don't forget to pick up the rest of your clothes while you're there. She has a few more everyday outfits and a Sunday best for you to wear and undergarments too. I'm sorry it took so long to get you these things. I couldn't have you wear what's in your mother's trunk because of suspicions, but I can't have you wandering the house naked or smelling like a horse in church either. It's not a lot but I hope they are to your liking. Emily helped pick them out so they would fit the fashions in town. These things should cover you for now and we can get more later, or you can make your own things later. I have fabric bought as well. I don't know what skills you have aside from your gifts, but we should probably try and get you to attend the quilting bee in your free time, so you can do more than just cook and stitch basic clothing pieces. Though cooking seems to be your biggest strength." He replied patting his belly smiling.

"Again, thank you so much. I am very grateful to you." She kissed the top of his head and he smiled at her. He could see she couldn't be happier or feel safter with anyone more right now by how she acted around him. He was her home and her safety. She was his light and his second chance at fixing his mistakes from the first war.

"You're very welcome my dear. Now run into town first thing in the morning. I've got those chores covered. Take the cart to carry your clothes and hurry back. You need rest for the social later tomorrow night so get to sleep now." He left one candle beside her bed and took one from the hall table with him. He was glad to have her around, but he wished it was under better circumstances. Knowing that death could also be her fate, made him feel sick. He grew to love her more every day. Even though they were related, and she was about to find more relations soon, he knew that keeping her identity secret and safe was the main priority. He would tell her who he was later if she didn't find out in the morning.

Felicity

F elicity woke up with the sun. She was excited about the social tonight, but even more excited about going into town to get new things to wear. She wasn't a vain person, but she did enjoy clothes and fashion as many other girls her age did. The one good thing about being in hiding is that she could have a bit more fun now than when she was living in the Mage Kingdom. Domandunn was horrid with very few social events outside of wars and battles. King Hadrion never allowed anything good, just training the men for war and the women to bring medical aid to the men when they came home and on the field.

She had to keep her powers secret, study magic constantly, and she was always surrounded by negativity because of the King's intolerance to the rest of the world. She was frustrated that she couldn't help her mother in the first war. Felicity had not been let in on the secrets her mother had, and she was most likely not allowed to know where the dragons were, though her mother seemed to know about that.

She had been far too young and undertrained at the time. The war lasted longer than the battles when they returned home, too. The King ordered every one of his soldiers to travel and collect any dragon eggs that they could find. They were to capture any living dragons and bring them to him, where they were to be enslaved and used to destroy other towns and villages. Hadrion believed that the dragons would help him make a world ruled by Mage's and darkness. However, dragons by nature aren't mean, but when they are nesting or provoked, they can be. He had provoked them, and they wanted to attack him. He tried to enslave them, taking their eggs as collateral so they would obey him. Her mother tried to free the dragons that were caught and to hatch the eggs of the dragons that were yet to be born so it would be easier for them to escape. But, when her mother tried, she was captured and nearly lost to the world. She had escaped one night. No one knew where she had gone.

When the King found out, the world went into another war, but this time, inside Domandunn. The whole kingdom was split and some of the mage people were wiped out. The dragons that were left, and their young, were killed in battle, though a few had escaped into the northern mountains. That was how Felicity got the dragon egg. There was a female somewhere, who had to leave an egg behind, and Felicity's mom had saved it and brought it back to her. She wanted to find the mother, but she had been moved by the time she went searching for her. It would be hard to know where to look without knowing what dragon it was. The skill of dragon scrying was something she was not privy to in this moment. Wherever the dragon was hiding, it was away from the King, which was a relief. Felicity had hoped that the dragon had moved to safety. She lifted the floorboards under her bed. She had placed the dragon's egg there in a pile of hay where it would be kept warm and protected. The egg shook a little and Felicity knew it wanted to hatch buy wouldn't until it was safe to and with its owner. It was safe there where she could protect it for now, but dragons can sense danger approaching even in their eggs. This one could feel it now.

Felicity looked out her window and saw Tom shoving at a stubborn pig who wouldn't get back in its pen. There were some stubborn animals on this farm, and it made Felicity laugh just watching Tom chase them about, shouting at them. She grabbed her shawl and headed down the stairs where Wilbur had the cart and horse ready for her to take into town. He trusted her to go alone but told her that he would be watching the clock just in case something happened. He also told her Tom would be at the ready to save her... just in case.

"Here's some extra money in case you need anything else." Wilbur said, hugging her. He also lifted a canvas blanket in the back of the cart to reveal a sword. "As a back up to your adventure." He looked serious now. Felicity had been somewhat trained in combat thanks to Dormandu and King Hadrion's insanity, just as everyone was to some degree, but her main study was healing as the women were forced to. She could stand on her own should she have to fight anyone, and Wilbur knew this. She was just as feisty as her mom.

"Thank you, uncle." She replied, hugging him tightly. She laughed as Tom fell in the mud, while the pig escaped again. Laughing, she hopped up into the driver's seat and took off. The town wasn't that far away, and she was excited to go. She had only been twice with Wilbur and Tom, but since she hadn't been found out yet, he was giving her more freedom to go out and explore. Felicity was letting her guard down and she knew it, but she couldn't help it. She was enjoying this life and wished that she was able to keep it, but she could sense things were about to change. Maybe it was magic, or maybe plain fear, but she knew that something was approaching rapidly, and she had to be ready for it. They all did. Her stomach felt full of butterflies and she wasn't sure if it was fear, excitement, or both.

She pulled up to the haberdashery and hopped down from the cart, untangling her skirt as it caught on a piece of wood. A common struggle for the women that she wished would just disappear. She opened the door to the shop and a small bell rang.

"Come in, I will be with you shortly." A woman with her hair pulled up into a twisted design called out. She was working behind a curtain with another woman who was in there for some sort of fitting.

Felicity walked around the small shop. There were all manner of odds and ends for sewing and clothing making. She could see the fresh wool threads and the different colored fabrics, some plain, while others were dyed in beautiful colors. A few even had patterns! Felicity admired the odds and ends that were in various barrels and bins. She wanted to sew beautiful things badly, but that had never been an option for her as it was for others, since the only sewing she did was on men as they came back from the war. Her fifteen-year-old self didn't want that job but had to take it or die at the hands of a wicked king. She cringed at the thought. She admired the boxes of buttons that were behind the counter and stuck her hand in a barrel of plainer buttons that was next to the register. Their cold, hard shapes leaving imprints on her mind. She promised herself that when she was able, she would put nice buttons on everything Wilbur wore. He deserved it. When the woman finished up with her customer who left the store and turned to Felicity.

"Hello. What can I help you with my dear?" She asked.

"I was told to come here and meet with..." She forgot the girl's name.

"Oh, you must be Felicity. Yes. You were supposed to meet with my daughter Emily, but she had to run out for a bit. She's getting ready to go to the social tonight too. Wilbur had me make your dress. I hope you like it. He said you were roughly the same size as your mother was so I could use her measurements to make your dress. And don't worry, I know your secret and it's safe with me." She winked at Felicity.

"You knew my mother?" She was feeling nervous. She didn't know if she could trust this woman yet, but Wilbur obviously did, and she trusted him. She decided to do the same.

"Yes. Wilbur is my older brother. I know everything. I won't spill the tea to a single soul. You have my word on that. I had to make do not knowing what you were going to look like since I couldn't assume that you looked like your mom, given the changes and all. But I think that the dress will look lovely on you. I do have your other dresses here," she said pulling out a few large boxes, "and we can fit you for a corset now. Just come to the back with me and I can measure you properly. I will have the fabric delivered soon with the notions and bits tomorrow."

Felicity nodded then followed her. The back room had wooden dress forms all around, a mirror for fittings, and a few chairs covered in fabrics. Felicity stood still while she got measured, laughing as the tape measure went under her arms and tickled her.

"Wilbur described you to me, but you are much prettier than he let on. I know that these dresses will look nice on you for certain now." She completed her last measurements. "I have a premade corset that might just fit you, possibly two. We can never tell when someone will need one fast, so I have my daughters practice making them and at least one is just your size." She handed a white corset to Felicity to try on. She helped her adjust it. It fit her better than her old corset which she kept with her after running away from her home.

Felicity put it on and moved around. "It fits perfectly." She replied. It was comfortable enough to sleep and work in. Not too restrictive. It was almost like it was made by magic.

"Wonderful! I will let Alyssa know she did a good job. She's my eldest and about to be married to Eric, the blacksmith's son. I hope she still plans to work here when she's married. She is my best seamstress. I know Eric plans to work for his father still. They have a nice farm that he built next to his father's home. They won't need lots of land, just enough for food and the basics. The blacksmith trade here is incredibly busy. They might be the richest family in town." She beamed with pride.

"It sounds like a great match then!" Felicity replied, standing on a wooden stool, still in her underclothes.

"Oh, I forgot, my name is Margot. I get to chattering away sometimes and I rarely introduce myself because we have so many travelers in Imyr but none ever stay. We aren't exactly a large city after all. But I am glad you're here. Just wish I could see you in your true form. Your mother was a beauty. I bet your true form reflects that too. I miss her dearly." She handed Felicity one of her new dresses to put on. "I figured you'd want to wear one of these. I can pack up your old dress for the trip home."

"Thank you. And many said I looked just like her when I was younger. I hope to go back to my true form one day soon." Felicity said.

"I hope so too. But after that first war, I think you have many days ahead of you. At least you'll be dressed much better now. I have no doubt that Wilbur has you wear sack cloth more than anything else." She nodded to the old dress Felicity had been wearing. It was indeed one of her sack cloth dresses since her good one was on the drying line at home.

"I don't mind it so much. I really like the quieter life. I just want to be me though. I hate being in hiding." Felicity felt sad for her old self. She missed being seen in her true form. Even though Tom thought she was a beauty as she was, she wondered if he would still think so if she was grey-eyed and fair or find her less attractive as something other than a mortal.

"I can imagine so. Your mother enjoyed that life too, but she had to come out of hiding and fight to protect an entire race of dragons and the world. I think she did the right thing. It wasn't easy and many mistakes were made during the war, but she did her best and that's all anyone can ask of her... and of you when the time comes." Margot said.

"What mistakes? And me?" Felicity asked.

"Yes. There is a lot that goes into a war that you couldn't understand as a youth. Wilbur loved your mom so very much and was torn apart at her death. It must be slightly heartbreaking for him now, to know that you are all that's left of her line... and, well nevermind." She stopped and wiped at a tear forming in the corner of her eyes. She fussed around with the packages and put them on the front counter. "It doesn't matter yet, though. It's not the time or place to discuss it. I know it's hard but put it out of your mind and plan to enjoy the social tonight. You are young and this is the time for you to enjoy things. You'll know the truth when the time comes for you to hear it. You aren't ready yet..." She paused, "...and neither is your dragon." She whispered that last part so Felicity wouldn't hear it. She had said too much already.

Felicity took her things and loaded them in the cart with Margot's help. Then she took off towards the farm, head full of thoughts about war and what her mother was really doing when she died. She wondered how Wilbur and Margot fit into all of this. She was confused and anxious to get back to Tom and Wilbur before tonight. The feeling of dread was growing inside her and she knew that she only had today to live because she had no idea what would happen tomorrow.

Felicity

Once Felicity was home, she felt a bit more at peace. She was excited at the thought of attending the social tonight. She hadn't been out in public that much since living with Wilbur. She knew that the Mage King Hadrion and her ex-fiancé Tristan were out to get her now. Tristan was the worst, and she was glad to finally be rid of him. Especially now that she was falling for Tom. At home, Wilbur asked her to take some eggs to Margot's home as a thank you payment for the clothing, just a few minutes up the road. She already had the carriage out, so she dropped off her packages and grabbed the eggs from Tom, who packed them in a cloth inside a basket. She had just pulled up to the house four farms away when she heard someone shout.

"I don't know who that is!" A woman called out.

"You do! I know you do. Someone here does. You must have seen her!" Felicity got goosebumps on her arms and legs. She recognized that voice. Tristan. Felicity slowed her carriage down.

"I swear to you that I don't. I haven't seen very many new girls in town. Our town is very close knit. I would have known. Please, you must let me go!" The girl yelled. Felicity got off her cart and hid. She had to trust in her magic more than anything else right now. If she let anything slip, she would be caught and enslaved. Then what would happen to the dragon egg she had in her room? She saw a blonde girl surrounded by men on horseback, in the back field of the home she was delivering too. She was shocked they hadn't heard her carriage pull up. She had to save her. Time to act.

She took a breath and called out, "Ah! Just the person I was looking for. Come now. Your mother is waiting for you. She asked me to fetch you. Hop in." She motioned to her carriage. At first, the woman looked perplexed, but seeing as how the men were also confused and not ready to argue with someone else, she played along.

"Yes, I have a fitting to attend to. My cousin sent someone to me. I am late." She turned to the men, "Please, don't make me be late. I fit dresses and I haven't seen a new girl in town. If I do, I will tell you." She acted more confident then the victim she had been before.

"FINE! Get out of here the lot of you! I don't have time to waste with ugly girls. I have to find Andromeda." Tristan said. Felicity's blood ran cold hearing her old name. She hated the way he said it. It was no longer sweet and loving, but angry and harsh. She felt as if she'd been punched in the stomach and wanted to cry but kept her tears in and waited for the girl to climb onto the seat of the cart.

"Yes, let's be off." She said to the woman. The men watched them as Felicity turned the carriage around and headed back into town, "You must be Emily." She said, finally remembering the name of Margot's daughter, the one she was to meet for a fitting.

"I am. How did you know?" She asked.

"The rapid response of needing to get to a fitting gave you away and Wilbur told me it was your house. I'm Felicity. I'm Wilbur's niece. I was the one that needed to meet with you today. I can take you to your mother. She fitted me in your absence. I was to bring you more eggs as part of payment for the clothing. I suppose that can wait now." Felicity said.

"Oh! I am so sorry. I was rushing back home to grab some things for the social tonight, but then those men stopped me asking about a witch named Andromeda and even if I knew who she was, I wouldn't have told those nasty men. They are horrible and harsh. What they want with her, I will never know. But thank you so much for saving me back there. I owe you so much." She said.

"I know of Andromeda, and she is protecting the dragons from them. They want to use the dragons to take over the entire world. It's a good thing you said nothing. Never tell them anything. No one can find her. I don't even know where she is." Felicity lied, just this much in case Emily was not as trustworthy as Felicity felt she was.

"My mother said something similar too. Though I think she knows Andromeda but refuses to confirm. I think she's trying to protect me." She looked down at the hem of her skirt for a moment. "So, they really will kill us all then?" Emily asked.

"If that is what Prince Tristan said, then yes. He will kill everyone in search for his ex-lover and will kill us all." Felicity slowed the cart down in front of the dress shop, where she knew Emily would be safer. "Go in and say nothing except for Tristan being here and that you and I met on the road, and we became friends. We can't stir up too much trouble now, can we?" Felicity smiled at her new friend, and she laughed.

"Right. Because we don't need a repeat of this afternoon." Emily said, hopping out of the cart. She turned and waved at Felicity.

"Great! See you at the social tonight then." Felicity replied as she watched Emily go into the haberdashery and out of the way of danger. She wondered where Tristan and his men were going next.

Wilbur

"UNCLE! UNCLE! HURRY QUICK!" Felicity shouted at the top of her lungs as she raced in the house with her new purchases in arms. Tom was putting everything away in the barn for her. Just as well, since she had no idea how to unhitch a horse and cart. She was frantic and out of breath, stumbling in the front door and tossing her packages to the floor.

"What is it my dear?" Wilbur asked, looking around making sure they weren't being listened to. He could tell by the tone of her voice that something was amiss.

"Tristan is here! I saw him on the way home. He had stopped Emily at her home and was asking about me. She said nothing and knew very little. I hope to keep it that way. But he is here. He and his men are looking for me and they want to take me back to the King. I can't go back. I can't risk them killing everyone or getting hold of a dragon. They will burn this place to the ground." She sobbed into Wilbur's shoulders as he set her packages down on the end of the table and hugged her. He remembered her mother doing this when she found herself alone and in danger. He hugged her closely before grabbing her shoulders and holding her steady. He tilted her chin up to look him straight in the eyes.

"Imyr and those in it, are well equipped to fight if we must. There is old magic in this town, and I think it's best if I tell you of it." Wilbur sat down with Felicity on a bench. He made her a cup of tea and paced the floor before sitting on a wooden chair.

"What do you mean?" Felicity asked. She thought only those in Domandunn had magic. There couldn't be magic in other places, could there?

"I mean that I am an actual relation to you. Your cousin, to be precise. But uncle suits me more now. Your mother, me, and Margot, are all related. Margot is your cousin too and Emily. When the first war happened, Imyr was a town of magic. We all lived in peace, just outside of the reign of King Hadrion. But when they heard of your mother's magical gifts, Hadrion wanted her and took her to live in the mage kingdom of Domandunn. She was pregnant with you at the time." He took a breath. "Your father, he was ill. She did her best to save him and you at the time. But when she was forced to leave under pain of death, she had no choice, and she went. For a short time, you and your mother came back here to live with me while we waited to see if your father would heal, but then he died, and she had to go back. You were small and to save you from the pain, she erased the memory of this place in your mind so you could forget about watching your father die. Soon after, she was forced into hunting the dragon eggs and caring for you alone. I told her you could live here but the King forbade it. He thought you were going to be special too. He forced you to stay and watched you constantly. Your mother left you with an older woman, Haegar, who was a sympathizer to your mom and her cause at the time. It was only temporary. King Hadrion found you and forced you back home along with Haegar, who didn't want to leave you unattended while the King was at large. At least, until you were old enough to learn magic. That is when your mother stopped trusting any outside people and she wanted to get free. She tried to get you out of the kingdom, but situations prevented it. She taught you magic in secret for several years, but then things got worse and Hadrion demanded more from her. She had escaped to my home for a few days, and I was trying to help her find a way out for you and Haegar, but nothing worked. One night, she tried to sneak back into Domandunn to collect you. King Hadrion caught her and had her killed as she was going back for both you and the dragon eggs that she had stolen. Luckily, you were old enough to care for yourself by then, a teen in human eyes, but an adult in the magic world. That is why you were alone for so long. I couldn't come and get you. I wish I had." Wilber's eyes were full of tears. "Your mother was caught sneaking in and executed for her crimes. She did nothing to deserve what he gave her. She was doing her best to save everyone." Wilbur finished. Looking out the windows again, he saw no one but Tom, who was feeding Jonas and brushing his mane. He looked at Felicity for reassurance that she understood him.

"That makes a lot of sense now." She replied, who was also tearing up and looking at the floor. Wilbur knew that he should have told her before now so as not to ruin the day, but since Tristan was here, it had to be done. She needed to know the complexity of the situation they were all in.

"I hoped to tell you another way, but since you are in danger now, you needed to understand. I wasn't going to say anything till it was necessary, though maybe telling you sooner would have been best, but now that Tristan is here, it seems that I had no choice but to tell you. But only for your safety and that of others." He took a deep breath, leaning towards Felicity. "King Hadrion will come and try to kill us all. He wants your powers. He knows you have them now and will do anything to get them. Luckily, you reached out to me when you did. Any more time spent there, you'd have been enslaved or killed like your mother. A fate I hope never to repeat." Wilbur was close to tears at the memory of losing his cousin. "Let us hope that whatever happens, the dragons and you, will both be safe. We can't let Hadrion have that power over the world. We just can't." Wilbur barely choked out those last few words. He stood up and started pacing around again. He knew it was time to pack her up and move her to another location. If they were found, that would be the end of everything.

"I have a dragon's egg." Felicity blurted out.

"You what?" Wilbur was stunned.

"I took the one my mom had rescued for us. The night I told Tristan about me and my powers, it was the night I found out about the egg. He doesn't know I have it. At least I don't think he does. He suspected I had my powers though, and maybe that's why he wanted to marry me, but I confirmed it, and he betrayed me. It was the last egg that my mom knew of from the dragon's hatchlings before most of them were captured or destroyed. I took it and ran as far as I could. I searched for you. Luckily, my calling spell got to you before I did, and you were able to meet me. I can't go back now that they know what I can do now. I have to protect this egg. It wants to hatch but I put a spell on it to stop it. I know dragons travel better than their eggs, but I can't risk it hatching yet. He can't take this dragon." Felicity stated with conviction. She meant business and Wilbur knew it. He remember that bit from both her mom and dad, but there was another thing she didn't know about and he wasn't about to tell her what it was.

"True. Let's use this time wisely. I will contact others who can help us. You focus on the social tonight and blending in. Act as though you know everyone here. Tom will help you. Blend in and see what you hear. But as for us, we must be ready for battle. I have a feeling that will start up soon." Wilbur advised. He started packing bag after bag. This meant that they were going to leave or do something tonight. The social was just a cover to keep her identity a secret. If they don't know who to look for, they can't hunt her down.

"Yes, uncle." Felicity said. She smiled at him weakly, and Wilbur knew she was trying to assure him that she would blend in at the social tonight. She went upstairs and got dressed while he stayed downstairs, sending a calling spell to everyone he knew who was on their side.

Tom

Tom would never admit this to anyone, at least not yet, but he was falling in love with Felicity. They had worked side by side for a short while, but he could tell that she was very much like her uncle. She was hardworking, brave, and ready to take anything on. She was also very beautiful. He knew he had no time to think of starting his own family right now, especially after his mother had died and there was no father to care for the children anymore. It all fell on him now and no woman he knew of, would take on such an expedition of starting a new home and raising someone else's children. He knew that he couldn't ask much of her. So, he admired her from afar. She was always rushing about doing chores and helping her uncle. She would run errands to the nearby farms for him on occasion too, and he would catch her helping some of the older farmers collect eggs and plow a field or two, when she wasn't busy. He loved that about her. She was caring and magnificent.

When she came back from town, he noticed she looked a bit scared and anxious. He offered to put the cart away for her and she grabbed her thing and rushed inside the house. He put everything away, but against his better judgement, he went to the door to eavesdrop. He knew that he shouldn't, but he couldn't help it. He wanted to know what had gotten Felicity in such a tizzy. He overheard Wilbur say that Felicity had magical powers. He couldn't believe it! She was in danger too; now that he could believe. He heard Tristan and his soldiers around, harassing people and trying to find Andromeda. She was in a heap of trouble from what he heard them say. Now that he knew Andromeda and Felicity were the same person, he knew he wanted to protect her. He wanted to be her friend and maybe more one day if she survived this danger she was in, and he knew that his sisters and brothers would be ok with him leaving. They were old enough to fend for themselves but lazy and rarely did. They were to go to the social tonight too, but Tom told them to stay home till they did their chores. It was probably a good idea now since there was a crazy Prince running around. The social would be a good place for him to talk to Felicity about his feelings and see how she felt. He was curious to get to know her better too. He already knew what he wanted for them, a safe future. Tom just needed a way to make that happen and soon before it was too late.

Tom went home and got dressed. He decided to let them come with him too. After all, it would look suspicious if they didn't. Tristan didn't need to suspect his family of any secrets tonight. He told his siblings to dress up. His oldest sister, who is just younger than him, was going to marry a man soon too. Since their mom died, she was not nearly as much of a helper and was very angry and bitter towards Tom. She blamed him for a lot of the bad things that had happened in their family. It wasn't his fault. People just get sick and die. Especially those who are older. He tried to explain that to her, but she wouldn't listen. She said that it was his job to care for her since their mother died and that he needed to give them more money and time and all sorts of things.

Tom felt guilty he didn't do more, but he didn't see how he could have. Their father abandoned them and then mother died and now it was he and his sister to care for the children that were left. She wasn't going to do it and now it was all on him. Tom told Wilbur that he would meet him at the farm that night and drive them to the social. He loaded up his siblings in their cart. He pulled his oldest brother aside and told him, "Markus, you must watch out for the family now. Whatever happens, please care for them, and step up into your role." Markus was now eighteen and it was time for him to show it. He promised as they rode over to get Felicity and Wilbur.

When Felicity stepped out of the door, Tom's heart stopped. She was breathtaking. He knew now that he didn't want to wait for her. He had to ask to court her tonight. He had to get to her before anyone else did. He had completely fallen for her and no one, no situation, would change that for him.

Felicity

Felicity noticed that Tom was staring at her as he helped her into the cart. She knew he was just as smitten with her as she was with him now. Wilbur nudged her side and smiled mischievously at her. This had to be partially his doing. As long as she and Tom had been working side by side, it was a wonder that they didn't form some sort of friendship if not more. She definitely hoped it was more. Because she was in a dress, Felicity got to sit next to Tom in the driver's seat while Wilbur sat in the back with Tom's siblings who were chatting.

"You both look very nice tonight." Wilbur said, starting the conversation between Felicity and Tom.

"Thank you." They both replied in unison, then they both blushed. Felicity could feel the heat radiating off her as she looked at Tom. He really did look nice tonight.

"You two planning on dancing together tonight?" Wilbur smiled, eyeing them both. They looked at each other then looked away, embarrassed at the question. Wilbur nudged Tom and shook his head yes.

"Yes. We will dance together tonight, if Felicity would like to." He looked at her hopefully. Her heart skipped a beat, and she was glad Wilbur was there to start the conversation.

"I would love to." She replied, smiling. Tom blushed again. Felicity could tell his face hurt from all the smiling he did.

"Good. Because you two would be a very cute couple." Wilbur blurted out. Felicity and Tom both looked shocked, first at Wilbur, then at each other.

"I am so sorry for my uncle's lack of propriety." Felicity rushed to say. She was embarrassed at his lack of propriety.

"It's ok," Tom replied, "he's not wrong about that though." This made Felicity blush. They rode the rest of the way in silence, red-faced and pondering their next moves. When they got to the town hall, they took the cart to the back of the hall where they saw men caring for the horses and lining up the carts. Felicity and Tom walked arm in arm to the front door, followed closely by Wilbur, who had his thumbs in his suspender straps and was smiling ear to ear. Tom's siblings followed and dispersed into the room full of people.

The music was loud and upbeat. Felicity had never heard this type of music before. Most of the bands in the Mage city were calm. They only had a few upbeat songs and those were played for the King only. They rarely had cause for music anywhere else as they were constantly studying magic, war, and sorcery. She liked the beat and couldn't help but find herself swaying to the music.

"Can you dance?" Tom asked her, noticing her feet tapping.

"Not well. I haven't really learned more than a few slower waltzes. We didn't have much time for that where I come from." She told him, though she couldn't hide the feeling of shame she felt for not knowing basic dances.

"Then I must teach you." Tom smiled at her before grabbing her hands and galloping off into the crowd. Felicity tried to keep up with the tempo and not tread on Tom's feet. She stepped on him a few times, both of them laughing as he swung her in a circular motion. Tom kept her close so she wouldn't bump into others in the room, and she didn't mind it one bit.

"I am so sorry Tom! I can't keep up with the pace. This is new for me." She said, laughing so hard she started crying as they bumped into another couple mid twirl. The other couple glared at them before dancing further away from the rambunctious pair.

"It's ok. I don't mind it. I'd let you step on my toes all day if it meant being close to you." He replied. Felicity blushed. She was falling faster and harder for Tom than she ever had for anyone else. Towards the end of the reel, she finally got the hang of it and was able to manage a quick box step and a skipping motion down the line of people. Then the song slowed down. She moved to go to the side, but Tom grabbed her hand gently.

"May I have this dance my lady?" Tom bowed down to her, sweet and gentlemanly. This was a side of him that she didn't see too often when he was chasing pigs and sheep around.

"You may good sir." She replied, taking his hand again, grinning.

"Wilbur is right you know." He told her, giving her a twirl on the dance floor.

"What do you mean?" But she already knew what he was going to say.

"I mean we do make a good couple. And I don't think it would be a bad idea to ask Wilbur if we could court. I mean only if you want to." He stumbled at bit at that last part. Felicity loved the idea of potentially marrying Tom. Even though they hadn't known each other long, she already knew he was the one for her.

"I would love to," Felicity said, but her face changed, "I can't right now though. There are some complications that you are unaware of. I don't want to hurt you or have you get hurt with these things. I want to be able to give you my full attention and heart." She looked at the floor, feeling painfully sad that she had to say this to him. She didn't want to think about the trouble with Tristan. That man ruined everything.

"I understand. It has to do with where you were before and why the prince is hanging around here, right? Secrets that can't get out and that you can't share with anyone." Felicity looked up at him and gave her a serious look. It was time she knew that he had heard a bit of Wilbur's conversation with her at the house.

"Yes," She whispered, "How did you know?" She was scared that her cover would be blown and if Tom knew who she was, would the same thing happen with him as it did with Tristan? She couldn't be sure. She pulled him over to the side of the dance floor to get some punch.

"I may have heard you and Wilbur talking. I was trying not to listen, but I was getting water for the horses, and I overheard you two. I am so sorry for eavesdropping. I just want you to be safe." Tom looked her in the eyes. "I know I shouldn't have but I don't care about the past. I just want to have you in my future. I hope you can see that." Felicity was upset slightly. She knew this would put Tom in a great deal of danger now. She marched off to get Wilbur. He had to know this as soon as possible. She left Tom standing by the table.

Tom saw her whisper in Wilbur's ear about him. He knew she was telling him what he had heard. Wilbur put his hand to his forehead. He said a few things to Felicity, and she looked a bit worried and upset with him. He didn't mean to cause trouble, but it seems that he had. This wasn't going well. He wanted to be with her, not put her in danger. No matter how good his intentions were, he was afraid that he had ruined things for himself with both Felicity and Wilbur. The two of them approached Tom, Felicity was anxious and upset.

"We will talk and explain. You should probably know something about this situation anyways." Wilbur whispered in Tom's ear. "Especially, since you are part of this new uprising now. We have to go somewhere we won't be seen or heard." Wilbur eyed everyone around the room.

"I am sorry Felicity, and to you Wilbur. I never meant to betray your trust. I won't say anything. I promise I didn't hear much, and I just want Felicity to be safe. I love her." Tom looked between the two of them. Felicity felt both annoyed and elated at the declaration of love that Tom bestowed upon her. If only his timing had been better.

Wilbur put his hand up to stop Tom from speaking further, "I know Tom. You'll understand more after the dance, when we speak." Tom nodded in agreement.

"Please, Felicity, can we just enjoy the moment?" Tom asked her.

"Yes. For now. But please do not hate me later." She said, dismissing Wilbur.

"I promise I won't. You'll find me to be more understanding than most. My family has nothing. I am not perfect myself either. I won't judge you or your choices. You made them for a reason. Let us dance." Felicity was falling more in love with him by the moment as they danced around the room. She knew he meant well, but she was still upset at his lack of privacy. Wilbur was over in the corner of the room watching them when Emily came into the room with her mother Margot. Margot said something to Wilbur, and they all looked terrified. Wilbur sent her off, motioned to Tom's oldest brother, said something in his ear as well, and raced through the crowded room towards Felicity.

"We need to go, now!" He said, grabbing her arm.

"Why? The dance is nearly over now." She felt an intense feeling of dread now. Could this be the feeling she was having earlier? She knew something bad was coming.

"Tristan is here at the dance now. He is looking for you. Come with us Tom. We may need your help. Your brother knows you will be gone." They raced out of the town hall and towards their cart and horses. They got them hitched up quickly and went back towards the house as quickly as they could, careful not to look obvious. Felicity and the others stayed silent through the ride, nothing but the cart and horse's hooves sounding in the dark. Luckily, the dance was over now and the rest of the people there would be going home as well. It was probably better for everyone to be home and not where Tristan could hurt them. Though, home or not, he was cleaver and would find them eventually. There was no telling what Tristan would do if he found Felicity. They got back to the farm and started packing food and water for Felicity to leave while Wilbur told Tom about her story, clear down to her message to him and meeting him in the woods followed by their close encounter with the Night Mares.

Tom

It was a lot for Tom to wrap his head around, but he knew that he loved Felicity and would protect her no matter what he had to do. This Tristan guy was Felicity's ex-fiancé, and he couldn't help but feel a bit jealous and angry at him for hurting her, but glad he did so he could be with her. He wouldn't let it show though, at least not right now as it wasn't the right time. When they got back to the farm, Wilbur and Felicity started shoving stuff in bags for them both. Tom was told to ready their two fastest and strongest horses. He did as instructed and made sure they were watered and fed before bringing them to the back of the house. Felicity cast a spell around the house to buy them some time while they grabbed food, water, and whatever money and weapons they had.

"I hope you know how to hunt and fight." Wilbur said to Tom as he shoved cheese and bread into a bag, handing it to Tom.

"I can hunt, yes, fighting, not as much, though I played at it with my brother and friends when I was younger." Tom replied, adding apples and dried meat to the same bag.

"You will need to learn quickly then. Felicity is in danger, and she has some magic, but it won't stop everyone from hurting people. She really should be saving up her power to bring back the dragon race." Wilbur handed Felicity the bag of food so she could tie it to the horse. Then he started filling up canteens.

"I will do my best to make sure that she doesn't use it except for in an emergency then." Tom replied. Wilbur smiled at him. Felicity rushed back into the room with a bow and quiver of arrows for each of them. They put them on. Wilbur gave them each a dagger for their boots and a sword for their waist. The rule he had always lived by when the war was going on was that you could never have too many weapons. He passed that on to Felicity and now to Tom.

"You both must hurry. I can sense that they are nearby. Get to the northern mountains and look for a town called Tarragon. That is where the dragons were from originally and there, you will find help to bring them back. It is a week's ride. Don't delay. Hurry! I will meet you there."

They raced out the back door just in time for the spell Felicity had cast to weaken. It did this when she was scared. They heard Tristan and his men ride up to the front door and bang it down as they mounted their horses and took off. They raced through the back woods as fast as they could, knowing that Wilbur was on his own now and that they couldn't go back for any reason. It wouldn't be long before Tristan and his men caught up with them. They hastened through the trees, being whipped by sharp branches as they went, ducking under larger ones that loomed out of the darkness. Felicity's horse stumbled a little over a large rock but caught itself and kept going. Luckily it wasn't hurt.

"Are they behind us?" Felicity asked Tom as she ducked under another branch.

"I don't hear anything, but I wouldn't doubt it. We must keep going. I think there's a village about two hours away. It's cut off by a river. There's a bridge about half a mile down though. I used to go there with my dad when we would trade furs. It should be safe." Tom said.

"Let's go there then. We need a safe haven just to throw them off a bit." They pushed through till they saw the bridge.

"Up ahead! Go to the gate and they will let us cross." Tom yelled. They road up to a large gate built around a large part of the river. Felicity thought it must go all the way around the town. She and Tom approached the gate where a few men were sitting up on top, providing security in and out of the town.

"Who are you travelers?" A man, balding and large, had climbed down the ladder on the side of the gate appearing at the entrance.

"I am Tom, and this is Felicity. We seek to stay in your town temporarily. We are headed to Tarragon. We need quick rest and food for the horses.

"You sure about that? It looked like you were being chased by those other men on horses from what I could tell." He replied, looking over their shoulders.

"How far away were they?" Felicity asked.

"They are approaching in a few minutes according to our scout up there." He pointed to a man with a telescope.

"Please, they are chasing us, but we need in. We won't cause trouble. Just tell them we were not here, and we will leave in three days' time." Tom begged.

"Let them in quickly." Another man, older than the first, approached the guard and smiled at Tom, "I haven't seen you in a few years, Tom. How's your family."

"Hello, Horace. It's just me and my siblings now. Both parents are gone." Tom said, looking over his shoulder hoping not to see Tristan.

"Sorry to hear that." He turned to the other guard, "Let them in Gavin. I know him and they won't be trouble, but whoever is chasing them must be. Let them in!" He shouted up at the other guards who cranked a giant wheel and opened the gate.

"Thank you! I will find you in the morning to discuss more." Tom said to Horace.

"I know you will, son. Come on now. The inn is inside on the right half of the street. Go and rest. You and your pretty lade friend." He beckoned them in smiling at them both, and they took off.

"That was pure luck." Felicity said to Tom as they heard the gates close behind them.

"Yes, it was. That was very close. We almost got caught. Guess my father's side job of fur trading was a good idea after all. It might get us in to where we need to be. Let's put the horses in the barn and get some rest for the night. I don't think Tristan will be able to get us in here." Both of them looked around, as if expecting Tristan to show up any second now. They could hear him at the gate as they gave the stable boy their horses, taking their bags with them. Then they headed into the inn, to check in with a portly old woman who wore an apron covered in stains from various stews and ales. She led them to a rough, wooden table next to a large fireplace, then brought them a large bowl of potato soup and some mead. Then she scuttled off to holler at a few rowdy regulars who had started a fight over a card game.

"You boys better settle down over there or I'll cook you!" She hollered. The men settled down at the sight of her raised ladle, chuckling at each other, guzzling large pints of ale.

"This will be a good place to wait the others out." Tom said, chuckling.

"Yes, it will be. Though I wish those men would leave or at least be less noisy." Felicity eyed the men who had started singing loudly now, hiccupping between verses.

"They will sleep soon. Don't worry. My dad and I stayed here often. They are harmless, just disgusting." Tom said to Felicity who was looking at a man and women sitting at a corner table.

"Those people are watching us." She whispered to Tom. Tom looked over at them. The man was lanky with blonde, greasy hair and the woman was fat with a stained dress and brown, frizzy curls all over her head.

"Yes, they are." Tom replied.

Felicity

The man stood up from his spot in the corner and approached them. Felicity placed her dagger on the table so the man could see that she was ready for a fight. Tom stood up to face the man, which was lucky for them as Tom was a foot taller than him and it made the man hesitate just a bit.

"May we help you?" Tom asked firmly, putting his hand on his belt and speaking directly to the man.

"I haven't seen the two of you around here before, and I know everyone that comes here." He said as the woman also walked towards them. Felicity could tell he was a regular just by the way he smelled of drink and smoke.

"We are just passing through. We will be gone in a few days." Tom replied, trying to stay calm. He knew guys like this were not easily swayed out of a fight, but that seemed to be just what he was looking for.

"I don't like you. I want you and your little hussy of a partner to leave tonight. This is my hangout, and I don't want no strangers here. Finish your meal and get out." He shouted at them. Tom grabbed Felicity's dagger off the table, ready to slice the man in two. Felicity grabbed Tom's arm and the man grimaced at them.

"What is the problem over here now Elbert?" The inn owner appeared with a wooden spoon in hand this time, wiping her brow with the other. She seemed to be used to his bad behavior and only put up with it for the money.

"I don't like these folks, Miranda. They look strange to me. I don't want them here. Make 'em leave." Elbert replied.

"You've had far too many ales to drink. Why don't you and Marnie go home and sleep some. You have work in two days, and I doubt that Andrew will want you drunk near an open flame. Go on and git!" Miranda said motioning with the spoon to Elbert and his wife, "Sorry about them. They are the town drunks, and this is the only place to sleep, drink or get into a poker game. I'd take it away from them, but men like him like it so much and it brings in the money without much effort. Hope you guys are ok and that he didn't offend you much. Clearly, he has such a way with words." Miranda rolled her eyes.

"We are fine. Thank you, ma'am." Tom replied, sitting back down.

"Please, call me Miranda. You're welcome here anytime you'd like. As long as there's not much trouble, you'll always be welcome here." She smiled at Felicity gently. Felicity liked her.

"Thank you, Miranda." Felicity said. She was thankful for her kindness and generosity towards them. She had a feeling this was someone she could trust if it came down to it.

"Welp, you two best be going up to bed. I am sure you are worn out. You brought quite a bit of stuff, so I am sure you traveled far and have longer to go." She said.

"We are going to Tarragon." Felicity said. She could feel a deep sense of trust with this woman.

"Tarragon! Well, I'll be. That's where dragons were first born from. I miss those poor dears. I heard rumors someone was trying to bring them back. At least that was what the fuss was about at the gate earlier. But that's just what I heard through the grapevine of an old inn and a few guards talking. You never know what to trust these days." She looked at the pair of them, "I hope that you guys get there safely. It is pretty dangerous out there right now. Bandits and, if the rumors are true, the Mage Prince is also out there looking for his fiancé. Apparently, she left him, and he is offering rewards for news on her." She dropped her voice to barely a whisper. "My view is that if she left that soggy piece of bread, then there must have been a good reason. No man is that handsome without having some daddy issues." She chuckled. Tom and Felicity both smiled at that.

"Yes, he is a problem, from what I hear." Tom replied, eyeing Felicity.

"Well, you two rest then. You'll be here a few days, which is a good thing, but once you go back out there, it's nearly a day's ride to get to the next town. Here in Guamere, it's a bit safer and most people stop traveling here. We are the only fur traders on this side of the river so many don't go much further. Tallwood is further along, and we get very few travelers who go in that direction. But if they do, they tend to come back robbed and scared. Make sure it's worth going where you're going." She said.

"It is. We will take heed and be cautious out there." Felicity said. Tom nodded in agreement.

"Alrighty then. You have a good night then and I will see you for eggs and bacon tomorrow." She winked at them. They gathered the rest of their things, and she led them to up to their room, where there were two wooden beds and a dresser between them. They put their things away and Felicity cast another spell on the room, one to make it more quiet as the men downstairs were still at it, and two, because there was a lot of enemies they had to watch for. She wanted to keep them protected. They both collapsed into bed, fully dressed in their clothes and boots, and fell asleep.

Tom

It was the second night that Tom and Felicity had spent in Guamere. They loved the place that they found and happy that could sort of relax and enjoy the peace and the running water. Horace had been to visit them their first morning and had been told all about Felicity and what she was doing. He was shocked at first but also amazed by it. He told them that he would keep their secret and that he would do anything he could to help them out. He also told them that he was once a keeper of dragons and would love to see them come back. That was news to Tom. He had no idea that his father was consorting with dragon keepers. And by day two, they had made plans to hear more about his adventures over dinner.

"Wait, so you actually helped a dragon get out of a snare trap?" Tom asked him one morning during breakfast.

"Yes. He was stuck and in pain. There were these horrible dragon poachers long before the war even started. But I had to help him. Male dragons are pretty rare. He gave me this long scar on my leg with his tail spine though." Horace lifted his pantleg and there was a six-inch scare from shin to knee.

"That must have been incredibly painful." Felicity said, wincing slightly. They could see the scar was so deep that it had to have reached the bone.

"It was. It took a lot of magic to heal it up as it was really deep. I was weak at the time and couldn't do much more than heal myself so I wouldn't bleed out. That's when your dad came to my aid and helped me out. He was a healer." Horace smiled because he knew that Tom wouldn't know anything about his father's past. His father had always been secretive about his life working with dragons, afraid that Hadrion would come after him to help him raise his dragon army.

"My dad did that? He never said. Why would he hide that?" Tom had to take a breath. He was feeling excited and anxious now. If his dad was a healer, what would he be? Would he have any powers of his own? He didn't know for sure.

"He was scared of the King. The thing about dragon healers is that they can do a lot more than that. They heal dragons of course, more like dragon doctors. But they can also help eggs hatch faster when they are with a mage of draconic powers. One of those mages just happens to be Felicity. And just like her mother, your father was being hunted by King Hadrion. Luckily, he was skilled enough to hide himself and you. He traveled a lot, which helped his cover. If they came looking for him, he would be here with us, trading fur. That wasn't just a lucrative hobby your father enjoyed. It was a way to protect you, all of you. It's just a shame that it ended so badly for him and for you. I know taking care of your siblings can't be easy. It will get better though. But I bet you anything, you are a dragon healer too. Maybe that is part of why you two are destined

to be together and to save us all and bring back the dragons."
Horace's eyes lit up when he said that.

"You know a lot about the dragons and have survived so
much. Why don't you come with us?" Felicity asked him.

"I would if I could. There needs to be someone here to
protect you. I have a feeling that something is about to happen.
We must all be ready when it does. I will be here late tonight
as it is my day of resting. I hope that you two will stay safe."
Horace looked around and eyed the corner where Marnie and
Elbert were drinking heavily and staring at Felicity and Tom.

"We will do our best. Those two will hopefully stop causing
us trouble. They keep making noises at night and banging on
our door." Tom rolled his eyes.

"There are troublemakers in every city you will travel to.
When I do my in-city rounds, they are constantly picking fights
with others, stealing things, making a mess, defecating in the
streets; anything that is abnormal behavior for good people.
They should really be locked up till they sober up, but some
rules here have loopholes, and we can't always enforce what we
believe." Horace told them bitterly.

"Is there no way to help people and get rid of those causing
trouble?" Felicity asked.

"Not yet, but I'm working on it." Horace stood up and
stretched.

"I think we best get to bed. If, like you said, tonight is
going to be a strange night, we better get some rest before
anything happens. Can't fight very well on little to no sleep."
Tom yawned. The lack of sleep was getting to him.

"Yeah, you better. I can't put my finger on what will happen,
but it won't be good. Pack your things tonight and sleep with a

weapon or two. Barricade the doors and windows. Only open for me if things happen alright?" Horace looked serious.

"Yes sir." Tom said. They went up to bed and did as they were told.

"Do you think Tristan will find me here?" Felicity asked Tom.

"Nah. But it's best to do as he says. He's never been wrong about his feelings before. He always seems to know if someone was going to get sick or hurt or be in some sort of trouble. That's why they put him on the wall. They know he is the best when it comes to protecting the city." Tom replied, trying to reassure Felicity but really only making himself nervous too.

"I hope so. I don't want to get caught. I'll spell the room just in case too. We can't be too careful." Felicity told him.

"Save your magic. You'll need it." Tom said. They both slept with their clothes on and their weapons close.

Around midnight, there came a loud bang. It woke them both up with a start. They could hear screaming and mass panic. There were loud footsteps on the stairs and banging at the door. Tom got up and called out, "Who's there?"

"Horace! You must leave! NOW!" He shouted that last bit and Felicity and Tom burst into action, grabbing their prepacked bags, and unblocking the door for Horace. He was there, sword drawn while everyone in the inn scrambled around frantically, dropping things as they rushed around with their bags on their shoulders.

"What happened?" Felicity asked him, dread filling her stomach.

"We are under attack. You need to leave. I don't have time to explain anything. Just get out of here. There is a back gate, but you have to ride through the city to get to it. Hurry. Grab your horses and go!" They raced downstairs, nearly bumping into Miranda who looked ready for battle carrying her largest ladle, threatening to hit people if they didn't get out of the way.

They kept following Horace out to the stables and hopped on their horses. They had already been saddled and ready to go by the farmhands who saw the trouble and knew people would be trying to escape. "Go! Ride to the far end of the town and stay safe, I must go protect the city. I will be in touch when I can. Head north." Horace took off and Tom and Felicity began to ride through the flaming stones and arrows being shot into the city.

Tom

The city was a lot bigger than Tom remembered. As he and Felicity rode through it, he couldn't help but wonder if Tristan was behind this. Tom saw Felicity touch the dragon egg that was in her saddle bag, making sure it was still safe as they narrowly dodged a large boulder that was being lobbed into the city. It struck a bakery, making the bricks tumble to the ground, and caused a fire with a loud popping sound. Tom and Felicity could hear screaming inside but they couldn't stop to help. They were weaving and dodging lots of people and it was slowing them down. Eventually, Felicity couldn't take it anymore. She cast a spell, sending a boulder and the arrows flying with it, back over the gate. There was a loud, unearthly howling sound, meaning they had hit their target. But Tom knew that sound from his travels as a kid. Trolls.

"Felicity," he called out, "it's not Tristan! It's trolls! My father and I saw a city attacked by some once. They enslave people. We can't leave them here." He teared up as they rode, breath catching in his throat.

"We have to! I don't want to, but we can't save them. The trolls will take us too and then what? We won't have to get out of here. At least enslaved, they will be alive. We can find some other way to save them later. Maybe by then, we will have dragons! But right now, we have to leave." Tom knew she was right. They kept riding on as trolls burst into the city, rounding people up in large cages. Tom looked back and wasn't surprised to see that Elbert and Marnie were pointing to them. They must have told the trolls they were there. Was it their fault that the trolls were attacking?

Three large trolls beelined for them and Tom shouted out, "Felicity, ride faster! They are coming for you!" He saw her lean into her horse and push harder and faster. The trolls were also fast. One of them caught up to them and took a swipe at Tom with his club. Tom dodged it, narrowly missing the end of the club by a centimeter. He had to get the trolls away from Felicity. He darted down a side street and the troll followed him. He looped back around to catch up to Felicity. They were almost at the back gate when the gate itself opened, but it wasn't for them to escape. Standing before them was another troll, massive and gird in thick armor made of dragon scales. Felicity and Tom recognized it because it had a green, blue, and red marbled sheen to it. Most dragon scales were that way.

"That must have been the reason they wanted to have the dragons! When they shed their scales, they can make an impenetrable armor with it! They aren't just their weapons; they are their source for war!" Felicity shouted as she and Tom turned down a side street. She looked behind her and noticed that Tom wasn't there. She started to panic. "TOM!" She screamed repeatedly. She didn't want to turn back but she had to. She raced back towards the gate. She saw Tom down another side street that was blocked by trolls. He was trapped and they were closing in on him, teasing him and mocking him as they advanced.

Felicity didn't have time for their stupid games. She knew that she shouldn't, but she had no other choice. She cast a spell and one of the nearby buildings crumbled on top of two large trolls creating a very narrow, but doable escape. Tom and his horse leapt over the rubble and back out onto the street.

"Thank you for that." Tom said. Then they raced out of the back gate, through a raging battle that was going on around the entire city, the heat of the flames on their backs. The city was in ruins and there was no guarantee who would still be alive and who would parish. Felicity sobbed for a moment and Tom put his hand on her back.

Felicity

As they rode toward the mountains, Felicity couldn't help but feel like she's had one too many close calls since Tristan found her. She knew he was behind the troll attack. He had to be. The only other enemies they had were drunk out of their minds and picking fights with everyone in Guamere. She highly doubted Elbert and Marnie were capable of orchestrating an attack on the city. As they rode deeper into the forest, it got quieter. They could no longer hear the battle that was going on behind them. Rain started trickling down into the thick of the trees, lightly peppering their skin with the water, which was just as well since they were covered in dirt and soot from battle. Normally, the sound of rain hitting the leaves would be soothing, but today, it was just another obstacle for them though it would help the others.

"Well, at least the rain should put out those fires." Tom said, looking over his shoulders where they could still see smoke rising into the now lightening sky. Though they were far from the city now, they could still smell the burning of wood and bricks.

"It's my fault they were attacked in the first place. We really should go back and help." Felicity looked at the ground and stopped her horse, turning to face Tom.

"We shouldn't do that. It's going to be ok. They will take you if you go back and then what? The dragons won't make it without you. You must keep going. We are so close to fixing things! You shouldn't go back."

"He's right you know." Another voice sounded just as Felicity opened her mouth to argue. Both of them jumped. A tall, lanky man, in his early twenties, jumped out of a tree, landing right in front of them.

"Who are you?" Tom asked, drawing his sword.

"Woah there buddy. No need to pull out the big sword. Besides, I was here first. That means you were trespassing on my quest, not the other way around." He smiled at Felicity but his stayed focused on Tom, who was hesitant on putting his sword away.

"Sorry. We can't be too careful. And what quest are you on?" Felicity asked him.

"I am looking for the dragon keeper. The mage that is supposed to rescue all the dragons. Judging by the conversation I just overheard, I think I found you. And don't worry," he said, "I won't harm you or turn you in. I was just hoping to be of service."

Tom looked at him, "Are you sure you're not one of Tristan's goonies? I will kill you if you are."

"You mean Prince Tristan? Nah, he's too pathetic to lead me. Besides, I'm a lone wolf. I don't need that daddy's boy. I'm Besnik, and I'll be your guide to Tarragon today. I assume that's where you're headed right?" They both eyed him suspiciously,

"Look, I get it, I am just a random guy in a tree. But I have been searching for you for days! I didn't know you had stopped in Guamere. That's how I ended up getting ahead of you. I was traveling through your town when Tristan showed up. I was going to come with you guys, but I saw what he did to Wilbur and the farm, so I stayed to help. I saw the direction you took and assumed you were coming this way. I was only a few hours behind you. Once Wilbur was ok, I followed. Now here we are."

"What happened to Wilbur and the farm?" Felicity asked desperately.

"They beat up Wilbur, but he used magic to protect himself pretty well. He only has a few bruises and a black eye. The farm, on the other hand, well, let's just say that the farm was set on fire, and I saved as many of the animals as I could, but they had to go to a neighbor's farm for now. Just until they have a place to keep warm in this weather. Jonas is fine, by the way." He said noting the fear on their faces. "I talked to Wilbur, and he will arrive soon. I'm sorry I startled you guys. I just want to help. I was in Domandunn before and trained by your mother, in secret, before she passed. I know, everything is kind of screwed up and crazy right now but trust me when I say I am here to help." Besnik looked at them both and Tom put his sword away.

"Fine. Come with us then. But don't cause trouble. Where is your horse?" Tom asked him, looking around the forest.

"She's a mile ahead. Probably not the safest place to put her, but when I saw the trolls and realized I wouldn't be able to do much about that problem, I camped up further ahead and hid in the trees, just to see what happened. Luckily, you showed up and not the trolls, though I wouldn't put it past them to come this way soon. They will go west, and we will go north, so that shouldn't be a problem as long as they aren't part of the hunt for your heads. We just have to get ahead of them before they find you." Tom and Felicity rode slowly beside Besnik as he chatted with them. Felicity enjoyed his company. He seemed nice and knew her mother. She could ask him questions about the dragons and see what he knew. Tom, on the other hand, didn't like him at all and Felicity could tell he was a bit jealous they already had something in common and a connection to her mother.

"See? There's my mare. She was a gift from my dad before he passed. He thought I should have a real horse and not a Night Mare like that dipshit Hadrion kept pushing on us. She is strong, though I bet she's tired after the week we've had. It hasn't been easy avoiding Tristan and his soldiers." He grabbed his things and mounted his horse, "Well, shall we be off?" He waited for the other two to ride ahead of him. They moved at a steady pace, hoping to stay out of trouble until they reached Tarragon, but as they approached the middle mountain road, they knew that they were in for a fight.

Tristan

Tristan had sent the trolls to flush them out. He knew Andromeda was there. He had magic, the same magic that she did, except for the special gift of being a Dragon Keeper. He could scry and find out where people were. Andromeda had a spell to prevent that, because she had been using it for so long, however, it was getting weaker by the day. She had to have known that. She shouldn't have counted on guards and a city of water to save her. He found her when she was asleep, and her magic was at its weakest. He always loved seeing her resting peacefully, though she never knew he had. Too bad she had a gift that he couldn't ignore. He had really hoped to marry her. He saw how Tom looked at her while she was asleep. He hated it. He added him to his list of people to kill. He still loved her, but he wanted to have her rule with him and take over the world, not just stay in their tiny little kingdom. He knew his want of power was greater than his want for her and the female flesh. He craved the world, and nothing would stop him or his father from getting it. Tristan would do anything to make her bend to him. He had to. She would be a great asset to the army his father was creating and the one that he would one day take over and make his own.

One day soon... He knew his father was sick and dying. No one else knew except him and their healer. If they did, they probably wouldn't be fighting the way they were. He wanted them to fight. He wanted them to see his power and know how strong he really is and know that he will gain control of all the dragons. They were nearly extinct now because of the last war, but he wanted to breed them like his father did and use them to control the other kingdoms and cities. He wanted acquisition. Why rule one land when you can rule them all and make them what you want?

The trap Tristan had set up for Andromeda was working. He had flushed her out. He could see his scout riding back, ready with news. "She is coming! Her, Tom, and another named Besnik. They will be here in a moment's time." He huffed, out of breath from his retreat.

"Good. Let them come. They will wish they hadn't. I will stop her getting to Tarragon. She will not keep the dragons for herself. She will be mine again and we will rule with our own dragon army." Tristan spat. He was bitter and he knew it. He was always told he was self-absorbed, and he no longer cared for anyone. The only reason he even cared for Andromeda was because she was considered the most beautiful mage in their kingdom and, if he was being honest, even as a human in her disguise, she was still very pretty to him. She couldn't hide that much of real herself.

Tristan got on his horse, ready for a quick and easy fight. There were only three of them. He didn't think a farm boy and his old friend from Domandunn could make a fool of him and his army. There were about thirty of them riding around in pursuit of Andromeda and only because his father wanted him to have his own protection, just in case. He didn't need it in Imyr and he didn't think he needed it here either. Tristan readied his men and saw Andromeda, Tom and Besnik come up through the trees, not aware of the battle they were about to enter into with him.

Andromeda's face changed when she saw him. It made him happy. She was shocked, then angry and finally hurt. He loved that about her. She could have all the feelings he didn't care for, in just a matter of seconds. This was it for him. It was now or never. The men engaged first. Tom was struck on the back and fell from his horse. Besnik was cut on the arm and Andromeda cast a shield spell around them.

"Well done my love," Tristan said clapping, "You finally mastered that spell." He knew that protective spells weren't her strongest point of magic.

"I had to. I needed something to keep you away from me. Leave us alone. You will lose, Tristan, either way. Just like you lost me." She retorted, angrily.

That was a slight stab and he felt it. "I don't think so. It didn't take much to knock your new lover down. I doubt it will take much to take him and my old friend out." Tristan spat.

"*Your* old friend?" She looked at Besnik. He looked at Tristan and then her and then the ground.

"We were. But haven't been for many years now. I started hating who he was and who I was becoming when I was with him. I refused to be friends with someone who treated others so badly. He had my family put in prison thinking that it would give him dragons. My parents were dragon breeders. I have the same gift, but I never used it. Once my father passed away, I stopped caring about what happened to me. My mother and sisters had plans to flee the kingdom and live in Imyr, so I helped them. That's when I knew I had to look for you. I knew your mom because she trained me in secret. But I also knew things about your family that she said you didn't know, and I was told to tell you when the time was right." Besnik was both embarrassed and frustrated.

"You were here to find me then." She said.

"Yes. But I had to see the dragons too. Make sure they were ok. They are, for now. But I fear that they will need a breeder in Tarragon." His eyes darted at Tristan who wasn't even paying attention to them.

"I understand that. Are you really not on his side?" Tom said, stretching his back from that last blow.

"I am NOT on his side, nor will I EVER be." Besnik said, more to Tristan than to them. Besnik's face was turning red with anger at his former friend.

"Ok. Then let's get out of here." Tom said. Andromeda held the shield as they rode out, Tristan stunned that they would just ride off, even though they knew he would follow them. Just as they were getting to the top of the mountain, arrows started flying into Tristan and his men. Andromeda and her group weren't hit at all, partially because the shield, but also because they weren't the intended target.

"What is going on?" Tristan shouted. Andromeda turned. Horace and his men were riding up behind them.

Tom cheered loudly, "What are you doing here, Horace?"

"Saving your sorry selves apparently. You can't just ride off without killing a few of them you know." He chuckled as he lobbed off the head of one of Tristan's men.

"Clearly. Guess you are here to do it for us then." Tom cried out.

"I promised your dad I would. Now get out of here quickly. We don't want them to attack you before reaching Tarragon. We will catch up to you after we take down this lot." Tom saluted him and he saluted back. They rode up the mountain just in time to see what was left of Tristan and his men retreat through the trees and back down to the city that was no longer smoking and burning.

"That was a fortunate event." Besnik chuckled at the thought of Tristan running away again.

"Indeed." Felicity replied, glad to be rid of the name Andromeda. She hated hearing Tristan say her name, it stung like a thousand bees, even though she had Tom who loved her.

Tristan

"YOU LET HER ESCAPE!" King Hadrion threw a vase at his son, who had dodged it and let it smash behind him. Hadrion had expected Tristan to collect Andromeda and bring her to him by the end of the week. He failed him miserably, again.

"I'm sorry, your majesty. We were attacked by the city guards who came to help her, and they all escaped. We were outnumbered and they were killing all of our men."

"That is NO excuse, Tristan. From what I gather, you didn't put up much of a fight with her, letting her shield deter you from a real battle. And to top it all off, she didn't try to kill you either, meaning she is either weaker than we thought and is trying to avoid a fight, or she is still in love with you, and we can use that to our advantage. You should have taken her easily. You have your own magic. Or do you still have a weak spot for her yourself?" King Hadrion said.

"She has a new lover. There is nothing left for me there now." Tristan looked at the ground. "I doubt we can get her to follow me willingly. We have to take her, there's no other option." Tristan replied.

Hadrion smiled, "Even better, we can use this new lover to leavy her heart and sway her choice on who to serve." Tristan had a bad feeling about this. He was heartless, but not as heartless as his father. He was angry, but when his father started something, he had to finish it.

Hadrion stood up and walked over to Tristan, "Father, I promise you, I will bring her back." King Hadrion shushed him.

"NO. You've had your chance. Me and my men will go. You stay here and play with your sword like a good little boy. You and your worthless desires for power, yet you can't get a girl to follow you back here even when you're in love with her. No more of that you pathetic child. I will do it and show you how to do it properly."

"But you're sick! And there is no chance of you coming back." Tristan hated being called a child, but this plan wasn't the best either.

"Then you'll get so lucky if I die out there on the battlefield. Then you can rule as you wish, and I will be rid of your stupidity." Hadrion motioned for his guards to follow him, coughing on the way out. Tristan was fuming. He paced around the throne room, angry with his father, frustrated with himself, and full of spite for everyone and everything. He was still in love with Andromeda, and everyone knew it. He was also growing in defiance against his father. How dare he speak to him in such a way? This was not ok. He was hoping his father would die out there while fighting for the power he deserved credit for. He had to get to Andromeda before his father did.

Tristan got more men together and went out to find her. He knew where she had been and where she was going, but it didn't give him an advantage. His father knew too. He decided to take a path that was a bit more dangerous but would allow him and his men to cut off his father's troops before they reached Andromeda, who by now, was probably only a few days away from Tarragon. He and his men raced towards the mountain pass, rocky and hard to travel, but the only way to cut off the others.

"We should go back!" A soldier called out to Tristan. Tristan was tired and sore, but he knew they had to press on.

"We can't. We have to cut off my father. I deserve this victory." Tristan said. He wanted to prove that he was worthy of power even at the cost of losing the only woman he ever thought of loving. Was he even capable of loving her? He thought he had been, but when he found out her secret, something in him snapped and he felt that power was more important.

"If your men die out here on this rocky path and the rest killed by your father and his men, then what of your power?" The man asked. Tristan rode up to the soldier and threw him off his horse. He drew his sword and pointed it at the man's throat.

"I AM the most powerful man in the world! NO one will live if he defies me. This includes you. You either help me, or you leave on your own, in which case, you and your family are banished." Tristan spat on the ground and the soldier stood up.

"Fine. But if you fail, I will say that I told you it was to be." Tristan cast a spell against him, throwing him into a tree and breaking the man's back before getting on his horse. Two men went to help him, but it was too late. The man would die out there alone.

"Let's move out now. No more breaks." Tristan had proven his fury was not to be messed with. They moved forward down the path, horses stumbling on stones as they went.

Hadrion

King Hadrion and his men were advancing quickly. They had very little time to stop before Felicity reached the City of Dragons. Tarragon was close and judging by the mess that Tristan made, they had a lot to clean up. Hadrion was angry about the trolls attacking Guamere. That was the dumbest way to find someone that he'd had ever heard. He always taught Tristan to be stealthy and silent. That boy never listened. If he wasn't the only child he had, he wouldn't let him become King. He would have had him executed for this disaster. Hadrion and his men were so close to reaching them. They had taken the Night Mares, the fastest horses they had. They were so close to her and her party. They rode up to the site where Tristan had lost his battle with Horace.

"They sense something." One of the soldiers told Hadrion, noticing the Night Mares sniffing the air.

"Yes, it's the dragons. Night Mares are notorious for sensing the dragons. This makes them nervous since they are the only enemies they have. Fire and smoke. They seem to go together but they don't. Smoke is what's left after a fire is gone and fire is the only thing that can create smoke. Essentially, the Night Mares are born of dragons and our magic, not just one. That's

73

why these horses haven't been created in a while." The soldier looked at Hadrion, impressed by his knowledge.

"Indeed, but only dark magic creates a Night Mare." Said another soldier.

"What do you mean, Hendrick?" The first soldier asked.

"In order to create a Night Mare, you must make a dragon breathe fire and then capture the smoke in a box made of willow. Then you take the blood of someone you love, drop it onto the top of the box, cast the spell, and the smoke transforms into a Night Mare. It takes all the nightmares of the person you love to fuel it too. That's why the queen hasn't been seen in such a long time. She is living her nightmares to fuel these Night Mares. The King has made it so." Hendrick spat.

"And so, I have." He replied. angrily. He knew he had hurt his queen to the point of her dying in a sense. She was a prisoner in her own mind and body.

A scout came riding back to their party, out of breath, "My King, they are up ahead, maybe three hours away. We should hasten to catch up. There's only three of them together. There is also another army that is following but I lost them. I will ride back to find them. They can't be far off." He replied.

"Good. Let's move out!" He shouted at his men. They took off, smoke billowing behind them as their horses rushed like a wave of darkness, toward their enemies, singeing the surrounding plants as they went along.

Hadrion could see the group up ahead. He knew they knew he was coming but he didn't care. Felicity must have scried them and their conversation before hand. It was a wonder since Tristan had messed up her capture so badly. It was as if he had given up trying to catch her over one small spell.

Tristan and his men were now hiding in the trees. Hadrion was angry. He told him not to come. It was too late now. They didn't need this many people for such a small, weak group. He coughed and blood came up. Hadrion spat it out on the ground.

Hadrion could see Horace and his men behind them, obviously trying to plan an attack. Horace had fought Hadrion before in the first war, and it was evident he still hadn't learned how to ride silently. Hadrion could see Tristan and his men get ready to attack Felicity again, but he failed to see Horace on the opposite end of the hill. *Stupid Boy.* Hadrion thought to himself.

Tristan rushed at Felicity and her party, while Felicity cast a shield spell, again. It was powerful, but Hadrion could tell she had been using her powers for too long to hide. He could see through her disguise though. She was getting weaker. Horace's men advanced on Hadrion. He could see the fear in Horace's eyes when he saw the Night Mares. Horace would know the history of them having studied magic himself. He would also know that they could burst into flames and blaze through an army if they chose to. Hadrion couldn't risk it though. He was too weak to get off his steed and let it blaze while he fought. And they were too close to Tarragon for any larger battle. If anyone in the city heard them fighting, they would bring out their own warriors but not the dragons. They were to precious for a small fight.

Horace charged at the King and threw him off the Night Mare. It wasn't hard to do with a deadly cancer raging inside of him. Tristan had been right about him being too sick and weak to fight. This would be the end of everything. Hadrion called out to Tristan who took a blow to the stomach from Tom. Tristan was angry with him. He could see it on his son's face. He begged him to help, but Tristan ignored him. Tristan slashed at one of Horace's men, cutting his arm. The man staggered back, and Tristan looked at his father who cried out again.

"Please, help me up. I'm sorry I doubted you." Hadrion pleaded with his only son as he was nearly trampled by a horse.

Tristan grabbed his dagger from the side of his boot, "No father. I don't think I will. You have doubted me my whole life. You took the blood of my mother to create your army. You betrayed us all for power. You turned me into someone who will betray those he loves for power. It is time to reap your reward." He stabbed him in the stomach and chest, "This is my war and I deserve the power and credit for it. I am the King now. The dragons are mine. You will *not* be remembered." Hadrion was stunned but he knew what he had done and that everything Tristan said was true. It became harder for him to breathe, and he could feel the life drain out of him. The battle that was raging on around him was becoming harder to see. His vision was fading, and his body was shutting down. This was the fall of the darkest King Domandunn had ever known. Hadrion wasn't sure, but as he died, he thought he heard the roar of a dragon.

Felicity

Felicity and Tom knew they were close to Tarragon. They both could feel it. When Felicity was growing up, her mother used to say that anyone who was there to aid the dragons would get this warm feeling in their hearts and be able to tell exactly where they were without trying. This meant that she and Tom were both connected to the dragons somehow. Tom found out he had the blood of a healer and Felicity was the chosen Keeper. There was only a small number of Keepers born in the world at a time. They could make dragons do many things, though Felicity wasn't sure what all of them were yet. She could also feel Tristan close by. They all stopped, listened, and looked around.

"We are under attack!" Tom shouted, just as Tristan and his men charged through the trees. Felicity cast her shield spell to protect them as they fought. Arrows and swords could go out, but nothing could get in. Each blow from Tristan and his men was weakening her shield and she wished she was better at defending spells. She saw King Hadrion just south of them, also fighting with Horace. She knew that he was following them, protecting them as a sort of guard, but three against an army was too much right now. She cried out to Horace, hoping that he would hear her. He did. He knocked the King off his Night Mare and rode over to her with several of his men behind him. He started slashing at Tristan and his men, trying to get them to back away so she could drop her shield.

"RUN!" He shouted at Felicity and the others. They turned and headed off towards the gates of Tarragon. She could see them, almost taller than all the trees. That is where safety would be. They hastened faster, horses nearly spent now that they have been through war and travel. Before they reached the gate they stopped, and a man on a horse called to them from the ground.

"HALT! Who are you?" He demanded.

"Umm... who are you?" Besnik asked, being his troublemaker self. Tom rolled his eyes and shook his head at Besnik.

"I am Thames, scout for Tarragon. I came here looking to see what is causing all the trouble beyond our boundaries." He replied.

"I'm Besnik. This is Felicity and Tom." He gestured to each of his traveling companions.

"What are you doing here?" Thames asked.

"We are escaping to your city. Prince Tristan is after Felicity for her dragon magic and Tom is suspected of being a dragon healer. We want to help." Besnik said to the man.

"Very well. Do you know what is causing that battle down the rocky path?" He asked the group.

"Prince Tristan and King Hadrion came to collect Felicity. Our friend Horace stopped them. They are fighting now, and he told us to run. I suspect Horace and his men will arrive soon." Besnik replied, "Horace and his men narrowly escaped their town as Tristan had it destroyed by trolls. We are just trying to get Felicity and Tom to you guys safely. There is a war brewing up around here. Might as well be ready for it."

"Indeed. Come with us then." He sent two of his men to ride ahead to confirm the battle below their city, while others stayed behind just in case. Going into the city of Tarragon was the most amazing thing that Felicity had ever experienced. There were tall, strong trees all over the city, stone cottages dotted between them. These people didn't seem to cut down many trees, so there were homes built around them. Thames noticed that they were looking around at the different structures and curious about everything there. This wasn't like the homes they had in other cities. Stone was hard to move and lift, and it wasn't very good at insulation when it came to harsh winters. But Tarragon needed stone. They had dragons who could breathe fire after all. Wood, thatch, anything not hard, would not survive in their city.

"Why is everything stone?" Tom asked Thames. Though he felt dumb after he had said it.

"With dragons around, especially new dragons, we would have fires every minute! Could you imagine rebuilding your home each time a baby dragon sneezed, or the moms became frustrated with their little ones? And before you ask, yes, we let the mothers hatch their babies even when they know the owners. The eggs will glow when their owner is near, but we want the dragons to be happy and not feel owned by humans. They are free creatures even when they find their human companion." Felicity thought that was a great idea. Mothers should never be separated from their children and she felt a sense of loss for her own mother now.

As the entered the center of the town, a dragon came lumbering down the street. Felicity saw Thames roll his eyes, "Serenity, what are you doing out here?" The dragon and its beautiful rider stopped.

"I heard you were going to find out who was fighting on the rocky path. I wanted to help. I am the trainer after all. What good is training dragons for battle if I can't actually fight?" She huffed.

"The point is not to fight. Just because they are trained, doesn't mean they are ready. You, yourself aren't ready for a battle." He told her.

"That's what you always say old man." She replied, rolling her eyes at him.

"I am your father and what I say goes. Take Lilith back home and wait for me there." He said.

"No. I'm going and you can't stop me. We will be just fine." Serenity and Lilith took off into the sky, Lilith roaring loudly as they swooped over the high gates, nearly knocking off one of the guards on his tower.

"That girl is going to get her, or her dragon killed." Thames said. He motioned to one of the city guards, whispered something in his ear, and the guard walked off.

"I can go after her if you want." Besnik replied.

"Thank you but no. This time, she must learn things the hard way. I just hope that Tom really is a dragon healer. We might need your powers sooner than you think." He looked nervous, but it was clear that the guard he spoke to was going after Serentiy and Lilith. That added comfort.

Dragons, Soldiers, and War

S erenity had reached the battle at its end. She had seen a man stabbing the Mage King. She wasn't surprised someone stabbed him as much as she was at WHO stabbed him. It was Tristan. He had killed his own father. Lilith let out a loud roar as Serenity engaged her. She charged through the men, friends, and foes, knocking them all to the ground and stunning those who were still standing. Lilith bounded up in the air, to give Serenity an arial view of the battle. She was fast and graceful with her light blue scales. No one had seen a full-sized dragon in years. The men from Tarragon had followed Serenity into battle now, stabbing the shocked men as they rode through. From up high, Serenity noticed one of the guards coming on his own, towards the battle. That was why her dad let her go. He was going to send another man after her this time. She shook her head as Lilith darted towards the ground, knocking people off their horses, and making the Night Mares rear back in sheer terror at their only enemy.

The battle waged hard, and Tristan was glad he was prepared to catch not only Felicity but a dragon too. Tristan and his men got ready ropes to try and capture Lilith. They threw their first rope at her and captured her foot, causing

Serenity to slip on Lilith's back. She slid down the side of her dragon, barely holding on to her by a ridge in one of her scales. One of the Tarragon soldiers rode by, cut the rope, and stabbed the soldier that had done it. They tried again, trying over and over to capture Lilith, but each time, the Tarragon soldiers cut the ropes, stabbed the men, and pushed them further back into the woods. Tristan was losing men left and right the more he tried. The Tarragon soldiers, while very few, were strong. Tristan had had enough. It was time for some darker magic. Tristan clapped his hands together once, rubbed them furiously while muttering a few words under his breath. A large, blue ball of fire appeared. He threw it at one of the Tarragon soldiers knocking him off his horse.

Serenity told Lilith to breathe her own fire at him. She inhaled and her chest burned red. She spat fire at Tristan which he barely dodged, and it set the trees next to him on fire. This time, he aimed his blast at Serenity and Lilith. Lilith swerved just in time to dodge the large, blue fireball. Lilith warmed up to blast back at the men, this time, a larger blast of fire streaming from her. She set the grass, trees, bushes, several of the Night Mare's tails, and men, on fire. Tristan had enough as the flame nearly hit him again, this time, he tried a new spell. He moved his fingers back and forth rapidly before aiming at Lilith. Small shards of metal flew from the ground and at Lilith and Serenity. Serenity tried to help her swerve away from the blast, but she didn't make it. The shards grazed her cheek and tore into Lilith's left wing. Serenity braced herself for a crash as they fell to the ground, causing dirt, rocks, and plants to upend all over them. Her father had been right. There was no way she had been ready to fight someone as powerful as Tristan. She wasn't prepared for this type of magic. Serenity was stubborn though. She refused to give up. The soldier that her father had sent, finally caught up to them.

"Please get home. Your dragon is hurt. She can't fight that way, and neither can you." He told her. She hated to admit it, but he was right. Serenity got up and wiped the blood off her face. She tried to coax Lilith off to the side so she could tend to her, but men were advancing on them, ready to tie up her dragon again. Now that they were hurt, it was essential that they leave. Serenity grasped her sword and pulled it from its sheath. She was ready to do whatever she needed to do to save Lilith. Several of the men bound her feet and claws as Serenity and two of the Tarragon soldiers swung their swords rapidly at them. The heavy blows of metal on metal were too much for Serenity and she was exhausting herself rapidly. Even though she had trained night and day, she was not an experienced fighter. Everyone in Tarragon had been made to train the second they turned fourteen, not unlike those in Dormandu. She was no different except for the fact that she was allowed to choose the intensity of her training unlike Mage's, who had to fight to the death. Serenity fought with all her might, but it wasn't always enough. Luckily, the Tarragon soldiers were strong enough to push Tristan and his men into a retreat. They were down to their last ten men, and not able to capture the dragon as they hoped, and since Felicity was no longer there, they had very little to fight for.

"I will come back for all of you and Tarragon itself!" Tristan yelled as they rode off. "None of you will live!"

"Good luck with that!" Serenity hollered back, limping over to Lilith.

"This will be war on all of you!" Tristan replied bitterly, turning his Night Mare around to follow his men back home. They had won this time, but they all knew that Tristan would return and that he would have a magic army to support himself by then. They had to hope that the magic that he used today would deplete his power and that he would have to find other ways to fight them.

The men got Lilith up and able to walk back home, though she was stumbling through the trees. She had taken down a birch tree and a sycamore on the way back home. Serenity was trying hard not to cry for her dragon. Her father had been right. She was not able to fight yet. She had to train harder than ever now. One of the soldiers told Thames that it was time to prepare for war and they needed to tell the Queen of Tarragon to engage in preparations for the war. Everyone else who had been in the battle already knew what to do. They headed to the smithy to get their blades resharpened and their armor repaired. Serenity took her dragon to the nest where all the dragons, and the healer, were able to help them. There was only one healer there, who had very little control over larger wounds now. He had been the healer during the last battle and his magic was spent on healing larger wounds. Now, he taught others to use herbs to heal dragons and save what little magic they had unless it was an emergency. There weren't any healers in Tarragon at the moment, the ones they had were not of age, but now that Tom was there, he had one person with the healing magic that he could train for this up-and-coming war. He called for Tom to help him with Lilith.

"With deep wounds like this, we must make a paste to cleanse the wound. It has honey and moss to protect it. A bandage if you will. Then place your hands over it like this," he put his hands on the wounds and Tom followed, "then say the words of healing over them." He chanted and Tom copied him word for word. The healer looked at him in amazement.

"What? Did I do it wrong?" Tom asked him.

"On the contrary, friend. You spoke it perfectly. You have a very powerful and natural gift for dragon healing. Shall we lift the bandage and check the wound?" Tom and Oaken, the healer, peeled back the moss and honey bandages. Tom stood up in amazement. The wounds were all gone but a small scar where she had been cut.

"How did I do that?" He shouted a bit louder than he wanted to.

"Magic from within you, compassion, and a bit of herbal medicine. It all works together as one. If you want to heal someone, you will. If you use your magic gift and a bit of the herbal medicine to assist you, you won't use up all your magic and you can heal more effectively. Though, for smaller wounds, just use herbal medicine. Using too much magic will deplete your strength and all magic has its limits, even the good kind." Oaken replied.

"Why are you no longer able to heal larger wounds then?" Tom asked, though he thought he knew the answer.

"The last battle was so brutal and cruel that there was too much healing to be had. I also used my powers to bring a dragon back from near death. He was on the brink, and I gave everything to him so my wife could have her dragon brought back. They both ended up dying a few years later, after the war. It was all for nought. My wife had been sick from battle and her dragon died soon after of a broken heart. I would have joined in too, but I was so desperately needed here that I couldn't bring myself to do it. It took me years to heal myself inside, even with my magic." Oaken looked sad, took a deep breath, and continued. "Now, I am here and will train you to heal. I will do what I can and guide you, but it seems as though war is coming soon, and we no longer have the time to work at it the way we should. We will be fighting within a month I assume. That is generally the space of time that is needed to prepare for battle. Let us hope that things will not end as they did before. At least, you have a natural gift for healing, though. That much is helpful." Oaken replied. Tom agreed and they let Lilith rest with Serenity at her side.

Good for Nothing War

Tom was training to be a dragon healer as hard as he could, night and day, and Felicity was no longer hiding herself with magic. She had hoped that the change would allow her to go back to her normal self, blonde and fair, but she had been hiding too long and the magic was too strong, so she stayed as she was. Tom didn't mind it either way. He loved her as she was and sometimes, at night, he would see a glimpse of her as Andromeda. He told her this once and it made them both hopeful that she could go back to how she was before. Though, both of them were too preoccupied with war that looks meant nothing anymore. Tom was scarfing down his breakfast one day before training, running a bit behind. He kissed Felicity on the cheek, while nearly knocking over her water goblet since he had his nose in a book on herbs and tinctures.

"Tom please!" Felicity cried out, catching the goblet before it spilt. Tom blushed red behind a small leather book he had been reading while walking around.

"Sorry. I just have to get this down before the war. They have only me and Oaken to heal those who come back hurt." He was feeling stressed and sick thinking about that. "If I don't learn how to heal arrow wounds, too many of us will die."

"I know. It is important. I have to go hatch a few more dragons and start training and breeding them right away myself. Not that they don't already have over three thousand ready to go with scouts finding more each day, but this is their version of plan A. I think that using magic is plan B. We should be practicing swordsmanship and archery right now. Then follow up with magic." Felicity was feeling it too. They knew that there were very few people that were openly practicing dragon magic. The ones that were, were in Tarragon, while others had to be sought after. Many nomads were hiding with their dragons in places that no one could get to without a dragon. They were the real protectors of the species. They were all afraid to be used for evil or killed off in the fight for good. No one could stress that more than Tom and Felicity as they were right in the middle of everything. They had met the Queen of Tarragon and she asked them to help her if they could. Felicity told her that they would do their best to do what she needed. It seemed like a good idea at the time. Now though, not so much.

"I just want this war to be over. Then we can learn on our own terms." Tom told her.

"I agree. Let's find a way to finish this fast." Felicity replied.

"Hey, are you guys ready for battle tomorrow?" Besnik came into the room, armored already with a sword on his hip.

"Not even close to it." Tom answered, not looking up from his book.

"Come on! Don't you want to see Tristan go down?" He joked, nudging Tom on the shoulder as he sat at the table.

"Honestly? I don't want to see anyone get hurt. I wish we could change minds with words, but we can't. So, I will fight like everyone else and be done with it." Tom snapped.

"Okay, okay! Just saying, you stole his girl, his girl stole his dragon, and he blew up your favorite childhood town where you would go to trade with your dad. You'd think there'd be some sort of revenge plot here." Besnik was getting on Felicity's nerves.

"Look, just because you hate everyone, doesn't mean the rest of us do. You left Tristan for a reason, yes?" Felicity shouted at him before Tom could say a word.

"Yes." Besnik knew he'd hit a nerve this morning.

"Then why don't you focus on you and your payback instead of trying to force it on other people. Just get ready to fight and hope that the only one that has to die is Tristan." She tore a larger bite than necessary off the end of her toast. Besnik sat there shocked that she yelled at him and impressed that she was following through on chewing that massive bite she just took.

"Okay then. I will go get ready. No need to bite my head off." He stood up and walked away. Tom burst out laughing.

"I can't believe you just told him off like that. Thank you." He said.

"He had it coming. He runs his mouth all the time and I am really getting tired of it." Felicity said, as she swallowed her toast.

"Yeah, well I would pay to see that again, and again, and again."

"And I would love to do it." Felicity laughed now too, and Tom dropped his book.

"Crap! I've lost my page. And I'm late for Oaken. Oh well..." He picked the book up off the floor in haste, flipping through page after page, till he found the one he needed, sitting back down at the table.

"Let's just finish preparing. Tomorrow will be the war to end all the wars, at least I hope so." Felicity said. Tom agreed. The rest of the day was spent training, preparing weapons, adjusting armor, and waiting for the call of battle. No one slept that night, though maybe they should have. The brink of war was not something Felicity had seen for herself, but it's what was coming non the less.

The Battle of Fire and Smoke

The day of the battle had finally arrived. In the early morning, before the sun had even risen, Felicity and Tom were up listening to the sounds of war. People were getting armor on, sharpening their weapons for the last time, and going over commands and instructions for different scenarios. This was it. This was the war of dragons. Felicity wasn't sure what she was expecting when the war broke out. She wasn't sure if she expected some massive fanfare, a parade through the streets, or what, but she didn't expect someone to knock on the gate of Tarragon and deliver a message to the Queen. Tom had been there when the gate was opened, and he volunteered to take the letter to Queen Fallon. She had been expecting this. It seemed as though it was from Tristan. A declaration of war. Queen Fallon looked nervous and paced around her castle, hoping to calm herself down, but it wasn't working. She looked worse with each step she took. She walked outside and called everyone together for one last speech.

"Today, we begin the war of freedom for our beloved dragons. They have lived with us peacefully, as we have with them. They are in danger of dying out if we don't preserve their freedom, and worse, they would be used to assault the world with fire and flame. We cannot allow this Tristan to take hold of them." She spat Tristan's name out as though it were poison. "We must fight to the death if need be. Though I hope that you, my people, will protect each other and fight to keep us all alive. Remember that this is not the first time we have fought and won, and it won't be the last. Heal each other, protect each other, and when fighting, remember that no one wants war, but it has been thrust upon us." She held up the letter from Tristan. "This declaration of war has the official seal of King Hadrion, though his son Prince Tristan leads it. We are to fight, and we WILL WIN!" She shouted. The crowd burst into cheers of a victory not yet won.

"Are you okay?" Tom asked Felicity, who was fidgeting next to him.

"Just nervous is all. I have a very bad feeling about this war." She replied, twisting her fingers together.

"It will be alright." Tom took her hands in his and kissed them softly. She seemed to relax, nodded her head in agreement, and put her focus back on Queen Fallon.

"We will sacrifice many things today, but it will be worth it to save generations that raise dragons for good. To those who are not fighting today, please go to your assigned stations. Children and caregivers must go to the stronghold. Let's get ready for war!" As she finished her last words, a sharp scream pierced the crowd.

"What has happened?" Fallon shouted.

"An arrow! Someone shot an arrow!" A woman who had been standing next to an older man in armor shouted.

"So, it begins." Fallon said. Everyone rushed quickly to their stations. The guards at the gate were already ringing the bell to alert everyone to the danger. Children were crying as those who were set up to protect them were rushing them away from their families. Besnik and Tom stayed near Felicity who was helping up an older woman that had fallen in the rush.

"We need to stick together now." Besnik said to the others. They rushed around and found Horace who had finally caught up to them after that last fight, calm as ever, telling people where to go as if he were directing a ballet not a battle.

"Get to that high tower on the east end of the wall. Take fifty men and start firing at the side wing. They can't get in through any door here. Get the archers to the wall and see Thames, he has set up the left side guard." He shouted to various men who came to him for orders.

"Horace!" Felicity shouted as she ran to him. She felt a lot safer with him around.

"Oh, there you are. Let's get you guys to your positions too. Tom, you need to go to the hospital. Felicity, you are staying with Besnik. He will take you to the Queen to stay there until you are needed." Horace wasn't going to mix words now. He knew Felicity would be upset about staying out of the battle, but they had to save her power and keep her safe. Her power was the most valuable of all.

Thames came running up to them before they could disperse, "Has anyone seen Serenity?" He huffed out of breath from rushing around.

"No. I haven't seen her since her dragon was hurt." Besnik replied and the others echoed in agreement.

"Oh no. That must mean that she's gone to get ready for battle with the others. She and Lilith can't fight! They will both die if they try." He raced off to go find her.

Felicity knew what Serenity was facing. She wanted to be in the battle too. The place was in complete chaos right now though and she had to follow the orders she was given. She and Besnik rushed through to the Queen's place where she had a war room of her own. This is where many advisors would come and talk through the war plans with her while scouts would bring more information so they could map out more strategy.

"Felicity, good. I am so glad you came," The Queen said, "No, Harris. We should move them over here to the east. That will cut off their catapult and allow us more space to charge and fire the arrows as our men push them back." She told one of her men as they studied a map. Information was coming in fast from the scouts and they kept adding and moving pieces around to create a more divergent plan.

"Yes, your majesty." He replied. She was very good with her strategy. Felicity sat in the corner until they were finished with their planning. Harris walked to the door to act as her guard now while they talked.

"Okay, now for you." Fallon turned to Felicity.

"Yes. What would you have me do?" She asked.

"I want you to take over Tarragon for me should anything happen." Fallon replied.

"What?" Felicity wasn't sure she heard her properly.

"I want you to be the Queen of Tarragon for me should anything happen to me in this battle. I don't want my people to be without a ruler and you are a powerful mage with dragon magic. I don't want anyone else to take my place but you. Are you up for that?" She asked.

"I... uh... I suppose so." Felicity replied.

"Good. Then sign this contract. I already had Thames and Horace sign it along with several of my other advisors who knew my plan." She set out a scroll of paper and Felicity signed both as Andromeda and Felicity and the Queen instructed her to tuck it in her shirt beneath her armor. "Ok, then off you go. I am sure you want to battle with your ex-fiancé just as much as the rest of us. But head to the dragons instead. Many will need your help there." She went back to battle planning with Harris, her advisor. Felicity walked to the door, shocked at what had just happened, but she couldn't resist noticing that the Queen was putting on her own battle armor and was preparing to leave soon, leaving Harris in charge of battle plans. She winked at Felicity. This was going to be an intense war.

The Battle Rages On

Felicity wasn't about spend time with baby dragons while everyone was out there fighting for her and the dragons to survive. She tightened up the armor she had on and raced out the door. There were people scrambling around getting more ammo, sharpening swords that have dulled on armor, and swapping out broken bow strings so they can get back into battle. There were people being taken to and from the hospital to get healed, and at least one injured dragon had been taken back, led by Tom as Oaken followed, mixing up herbs and putting it on the dragon's bleeding leg as they went. She had no idea where to go, so she went and found Horace.

"Aim at the catapult operators!" Horace yelled at his archers. There were men trying to catapult large boulders over the wall. There were others trying to climb the wall with ladders and ropes. The ropes were being cut as men fell to their deaths below. Then there were the Mage's. Tarragon had only a few that still had magic left, but they were there and ready to fight too. Most of them were casting protective spells on the city, while others were out healing those who were injured in the field since healing magic wasn't as unique as dragon magic.

"Horace!" Felicity called out as an arrow flew past his head towards the enemy line.

"What are you doing here?" He shouted, scratching his ear. The tip of the arrow's feathers had barely touched him.

"The Queen is out here fighting now, and I didn't want to stay behind." She replied.

"She's WHAT?" He shouted at her, making her jump.

"She told me she wanted me to be Queen if anything happened to her. But I don't want that. I need her to stay alive. I signed her contact still, but I don't want to be Queen. I want to be out here fighting with you." She was on the verge of tears. War was too much for her right now. She knew she had no choice either way, but this was more than she could handle.

"I will go and find her, or you may be Queen soon enough. Though, she is a very fierce warrior. She won the war for us last time and I don't think you have much to fear this time. Please, go to the dragon's nest and hatch more of the younglings. I know you don't want to, but that is the best place for you to be if you want to keep others alive right now. Speed up their growth and training if you can." Horace said, as he cut a line of rope that had just appeared on the wall. Felicity ran off the city wall, dodging men swinging swords and arrows that were flying past her. An arrow had narrowly missed her, sideswiping her armor. She could see the Queen outside of the gate, slicing at other men and casting spells left and right. She tried to call out to her sensing danger as two men approached her. One stabbed her in the back and the other in the side. Both had found the weakest points in her armor. As she climbed down the ladder that led up to the wall, she spotted the Queen being pulled back in behind the gate by several of the soldiers. Felicity rushed over to help.

"You should have stayed behind!" She cried out to Queen Fallon.

"I know. But I didn't want to watch my men die without saying I was brave enough to fight side by side with them. We ALL need to protect each other and the dragons." She choked out. Felicity could tell her injuries were too bad to be fixed.

"You can't die! We NEED you! I can't be Queen." Felicity felt sick to her some stomach. Tears welled up in her eyes and she was struggling to hold them back. "I need you." She whispered to Fallon.

"Everything will be fine. You can do this. Thames will guide you. And Harris. You need to lead this war now." She said, looking into Felicity's eyes. She started to gasp for air, blood bubbling up in the corners of her mouth before she shuttered and exhaled for the last time. Her hand went limp in Felicity's hand and the men took her away.

Felicity broke down crying while the other men who helped bring Queen Fallon back, went outside the gates to fight again. A few bowed to her now as they passed, knowing she was the new ruler of Tarragon. She couldn't handle this. She was only supposed to work with the dragons. She wasn't supposed to lead them. Now she had no choice. Fallon had left something in her hand as she had been taken away. It was her medallion. She had taken it off and given it to Felicity. It had the mark of the Queen on it. This must have been her way of proving she was the rightful heir to Tarragon now aside from the contract that was tucked inside Felicity's shirt. Felicity put it on. She walked to the nest where the dragons were. She was angry at Tristan and there was no way she was going to let him win this war.

Make Way for the Queen

FELICITY FOUND THAMES and told him what happened. He spread the word that Felicity was now the Queen, through all the different ranks. She had met up with Tom to tell him and Oaken personally, while Horace wasn't surprised at all when he heard the news through the grapevine. There was no one better to be the Queen than someone who possessed gifts to save them all.

"I don't want this job, but I guess I have no choice." Felicity was telling Tom as he made a paste for a deep laceration.

"Look, it has only been three days of battle and you had no way of knowing what was going to happen. You do have a choice though." He said pausing to mutter something under his breath. "If you really don't want this job, then I am sure that there will be some way for you to get out of it." He tried to reassure her but to no avail. Felicity was still anxious about her new role and to be forced into it by a battle she hardly knew the history of, she understood her importance now. She couldn't fight unless she had no choice and there was no successor if she failed. At least not yet.

"I know. There might be a few ways out, but I don't want to think about that right now. I need to get more babies to hatch." Felicity took off towards the dragon egg nursery. There were a few other people there that could train dragons, but none of them were keepers like she was. She could heal, train, hatch, and teach dragons the way that no one else could. She was proud of that gift. Even though she could do all of that, she still had no dragon of her own yet. Her mind wandered to the egg that she brought with her and the thought that she should bring it to the hatchery. She wanted a dragon like Serenity did. She wanted to be able to fly around on the back of one of those beautiful creatures and see the world from a new perspective. She wanted to have that bond with a creature that she didn't have with anyone else. She knew that she had to wait though. She had a war to win since losing the dragon race wasn't an option.

Felicity conjured a spell for a few of the eggs that were ready to hatch. She turned to one of the dragon trainers who had been feeding one of the younglings, "Are there any more that are getting close to hatching yet?" She asked.

"Not yet my Queen. These are the only ones. The rest are too young. We may need you for the war, so no one has wanted to ask you this, but you do have the ability to make them grow faster. We don't normally ask for that with the hatchlings, but maybe doing it with an egg or two might not be such a bad idea." The worker said.

"Maybe. I will ask Oaken and see if it's ok. I don't want to waste my magic if I don't need to. This is going to be a long war." Felicity walked out of the stable to find Oaken again.

"Oaken," she said once she found him, "Everyone keeps asking me to grow and hatch more dragon eggs and even the dragons themselves. What should I do?" She really needed to be guided.

"You should with a few but not so many. You need your magic. Magic always has its limits. You know that. The older you get, the less magic you have. The more you use your magic, the less magic you have. You are still young, but it's best not to waste it."

"You're right. I wish I had my own dragon though." She replied.

"You do, technically." Oaken stated.

"What do you mean?" Felicity hesitated, not sure if she wanted the answer. Things haven't been good as of late.

"There is a dragon egg that is off to the west side of the mountains. It's the only one that has been rumored to be protected by its mother. It is a light-based dragon breed. Blue in color and hidden in rapidly moving water by the falls. The dragon is a Moon Flame dragon." He told her. "The egg you brought with you belongs to another person that I think you might know." He looked over at Tom. She wasn't that surprised now.

"You mean there are different breeds, and you can tell who has what dragon?" She asked. She felt she really hadn't been trained for anything at all now.

"Yes. All dragons belong to an element outside of fire. There is light breed, which is sun, moon, flame, and lightning. The earth breed has rock, tree, and flower. Then you have air breeds like wind, storm, and weather changing breeds. And finally, water breeds which tend to mate with light breeds, and those are mist, rain, and river dragons. They are all pretty amazing to look at. The dragon that is technically meant for you can only be saved by you. It needs to be brought back here after you hatch it. That dragon would be the key to winning. No one has seen a moon dragon in years. They can do more than just fire; they can make themselves and their rider invisible."

"No one would see it?" Felicity asked.

"No one. It would be an attack that only you could orchestrate. I only know it's yours because it was once in Dormandu. It shook violently near you but stopped when the King entered the room. He knows about it and Tristan too. Though I heard a rumor that King Hadrion was killed by Tristan. So now, only Tristan knows. Your mother saved it and its mother. She helped them escape." Oaken said, hoping that she would ditch the battle and head out to find it. It would keep her busy and help them win the war, again.

"I should go collect the egg if it's mine. How do I get there?" Felicity asked.

"Follow the river west and into the large valley. There will be an open spot of rapids where the trees line the river's mouth. There will be a waterfall that is guarded by the mother moon dragon. She will protect her egg. Earn her trust and give her food so she will leave her baby and you will have to climb to get to it. The Falls are scary and dangerous. Tie a length of rope to a rock or tree and the other to your body. Repel down the falls and grab the blue egg. You'll see the light coming from it so it shouldn't be hard to find. Go alone. She won't trust you if you are with others. The rumor is that only the Dragon Keepers can get a light dragon for their own. You are the only Dragon Keeper we know of. This is your dragon." Oaken went back to work, leaving Felicity lots to think about.

Could she do this? She hoped she could. She wanted to. Rumors about dragons and their eggs were generally true. If this dragon could be her dragon, there was nothing that could stop her from getting it here. Felicity decided she had to go. She went back to the castle, now her home, where she began to pack. She went back outside, into the courtyard just in time to see Serenity and Lilith crash to the ground in a spray of stone and dust.

"HELP!" Serenity called out. Several men and Tom came rushing to her side. Serenity had gone out again even against better judgement.

"What happened?" Felicity asked as she ran up to Serenity's side, noting blood all over Lilith.

"Tristan cast the thousand knives spell. He shredded her up pretty badly this time. She might not make it!" Serenity broke down sobbing into Felicity's shoulder not noticing that she had a bag of things together and was ready to leave.

"It's going to be ok," Felicity told her, patting her back, "Go with Tom and he will stay with you and work on Lilith for you." She handed her off to Tom who saw her bag.

"Where are you going?" He sounded scared.

"I have to go collect a dragon egg that Oaken told me about. Trust me on this." She added seeing the scared look on Tom's face.

"Fine. I will. But be safe." He replied.

"I will." They quickly kissed as Tom led Serenity away to the hospital and Felicity slipped out the side door on the wall.

The Moon Dragon

FELICITY WAS SURPRISED that Tristan hadn't gone after this moon dragon before. It sounded like something he would have tried to take, just as his father had tried to take other dragons before him. Felicity hated them for this. She wasn't a fan of the king, but she also didn't like the fact that Tristan had murdered his father. He had been a good person before all of this stuff started. He had talked to her about a family and being in love with her and being better than his father had been before. Now, she hardly recognized him. He had become a different person the second he had told his father about her gifts, which she had told him in secret. She trusted him and the betrayal kept cutting deeper and deeper, the more the war raged on. She had no idea why power suddenly took place of the love they had for each other. But she couldn't focus on this now. She had to find this dragon egg. Even though the road was short, and she didn't have to worry so much about anyone coming after her, mainly Tristan who was still under the impression that she was probably hiding somewhere in the keep at Tarragon. She still had a long and dangerous road ahead of her. She had to climb up the side of the mountain to get to part of the river that was going to flow into the waterfall. Felicity had fallen a few times in between some rocks and scrapped up her hands and knees. She was no stranger to pain, and she did know that she was going to be doing a lot of difficult things to get to this egg as Oaken had told her.

Felicity had finally reached the muddy part of the riverbank and followed along it. There was nothing that would stop her from finding this moon dragon, even if it wasn't her dragon specifically and Oaken had been wrong, she was going to get it and keep it safe for the person it did belong to. Felicity heard the waterfall before she saw it. It was loud and rushing very quickly. The river itself was already fast moving and she had to be careful not to fall in when she drank from it. The edge of the river was slippery, and she noticed that the mud had some large footprints in it. That had to be the mother dragon that was protecting the egg. In order to draw the mother dragon out, Felicity had meat put in her pack, tightly wrapped, and spelled, so that it wouldn't attract other wild animals and that she would be able to sedate the full-sized dragon before scaling the edge of the waterfall.

She placed the meat on a large rock close to the waterfall, but not at the area where she was intending to climb down. She moved back into the tree line and waited. It seemed like it took several hours of her sitting there before she saw a bit of a dragon's face peeking out from the clouds. These dragons could make themselves invisible, so it was no surprise that she hadn't seen it flying right above her, probably waiting to see what she would do. The dragon looked around and then swooped down and ate the meat. It only took a few minutes before she could see her stomping around, realizing she had been tricked, also with magic, to fall asleep. She let out a large roar and crashed through the trees near Felicity, who had to jump out of the way before she got stomped on.

At long last, the dragon had fallen asleep on the edge of the river and Felicity was free to tie her rope to a tree and repel down the edge of the falls. She had to be careful not to slip on the rocks as they were wet and covered in moss and other things. She had trouble seeing where the cave was located and had to use a water parting spell to get inside. When she did, she found that the cave was full of stalactites and stalagmites that reminded her of the inside of a dragon's mouth. She created a fireball to light the way as she stumbled around, looking for the moon dragon's nest.

The nest was at the back of the cave, surrounded by a large pile of rocks. The moon dragon seemed to nest in stones, and she could see there was more than one dragon's egg. She wasn't prepared for that. Should she take more than one? They were desperate for help in the war and there were plenty of eligible riders and trainers who could help them with the dragons when they hatched. She also knew that most dragons would only hatch for their owners. Felicity dumped out most of the contents in her bag and loaded up the eggs. She went back through the cave and up the falls, where the moon dragon was still asleep. Then she slipped past her and moved up towards the head of the river and back to Tarragon. Was this too easy? Probably. Felicity started to feel uneasy as she moved through the woods. Someone was following her. She could feel it.

An Unexpected Surprise

FELICITY MADE HER WAY through the woods, back towards Tarragon. She had no idea why she felt like she was being followed, she just did. She hastened her steps to try and loose them in the woods, but to no avail. She could hear their pace matching hers even though she couldn't see them as they stayed in the thicket. She was running out of breath and the bag of dragon eggs was extremely heavy. She had to stop before the stitch in her side became a full-blown cramp and would make it impossible to move or fight. She came to a clearing and drew her sword out of its sheath with one fluid motion.

"Come out you coward!" She shouted into the wind. Nothing happened. She bent down to stabilize her breathing but listening intently for the slightest sound of movement. There was a rustling sound to her left and she stood up, ready to fight. She dropped her sword when she saw who had been following her.

"WILBUR!" She cried, rushing forward to hug him. He looked different. He was in a bit better shape, had on leather armor, and looked more like a warrior than she had ever seen him look before.

"Felicity, my niece!" Wilbur chuckled.

"How did you know I would be here?" She asked him.

"I had a feeling that once you got to Tarragon, you would be sent here eventually. They are some of the few people who knew about this place aside from Hadrion." He gave her another tight squeeze, happy that she was still alive.

"Yes, I was told to collect an egg, but there was more than just one." She opened the bag up to reveal the eggs. There were five of them inside.

Wilbur inspected the eggs closely, "It looks as though two are ready to hatch soon. We better get them back to Tarragon so they will have proper care."

"Hatch? How can you tell?" Felicity only knew hatching by magic, not by nature.

"When the eggs get hot and start to glow brighter, or they shake, or any type of change in the eggs appearance usually, it means that they will be hatching soon. These look more like precious gems than dark eggs covered in mud, meaning soon they will hatch." He held two up and showed her the difference between them.

"That must mean they know they are close to their owners." Felicity replied.

"Yes, it does. This means that you must be one of them. I don't know who the other one is though. I had my dragon, and it would be very rare for me to have another. That almost never happens." Wilbur replied.

"Then that must mean that someone else is close by. But who?" Felicity asked, looking around.

"ME!" Tristan yelled, stepping out of the woods, and going for Wilbur. He drew his sword just in time to block Tristan's strike, then he swung a counter strike almost hitting Tristan on the shoulder.

"What are you doing here?" Felicity snapped.

"I hadn't seen you in a while, so I thought I'd look around. Saw you going up the mountain pass and I followed. Had no idea that you were going to be feeding a moon dragon. That was fun to watch. Now, you have five eggs and I want them. Clearly one of them is mine. There's no way this old man would get a second dragon." Tristan said.

Wilbur made a face at Tristan and Felicity laughed, "You honestly think I would give you a dragon's egg, even if it was your dragon, after the betrayal and backstabbing you've done? That is the most ridiculous thing I have ever heard. Why don't you and your schoolboys go back to the battle and stay there. Maybe you'll get lucky and take an arrow to the chest. I would pay money to see that." Felicity was being malicious on purpose. Even though Wilbur was a mage, he was out of practice with his magic. She could see him trying to secretly conjure something out of the corner of her eye, though, and she wanted to buy him time to do it.

"Oh, come on now. Just because we didn't work out, doesn't mean we can't be friends, does it?" Now Tristan was taunting her.

"That's exactly what that means!" Felicity charged at Tristan, and he wasn't expecting it. He barely blocked her blow as she aimed for his head. She really wanted to lob it off, which made Tristan smile. He knew he had gotten to her.

"Really? You think you can kill me? I know that you can't. You were never one to amount to much. Not ever. You couldn't keep your family alive, you failed to protect the Queen, and can't even keep a man unless Tom counts as a man. Face it, Andromeda, you're not fit to do anything." He smirked. Felicity saw Wilbur motion for her to back away from Tristan as he aimed a spell at him. Tristan froze on the spot.

"You forgot one thing, my darling..." Felicity said, as she approached Tristan, "I AM the Queen of Tarragon now!" She brought her sword down and sliced of Tristan's head. Then she broke down in a fit of tears. Wilbur rushed over to her and put his arm around her.

"That was very hard to do. I can't imagine how you must feel. You are an amazing person who is about to save the world from great evil. We have more enemies out there and they are coming." He said, helping Felicity to her feet. "I know you loved him. Now you have your revenge, as horrible as it was."

"Still... I didn't want to do this." She choked through her sobs. Wilbur embraced her tightly and let her cry for a moment before delivering more bad news.

"There is another person, more powerful than Tristan and Hadrion and he will be here soon. We must get back. You know of whom I speak." He said reverently. "He will be let loose from his prison. He is the man that has done no magic." Wilbur looked at Felicity, her eyes wide with terror.

"You mean that myth is true?" Felicity asked.

"Indeed. He was a magical child that was born to a family with no magical powers. They hated magic. He knew he had powers but was too scared to use them for fear of his family killing him. The mages took him in but told him that he should never use his powers there either. They wanted him as a weapon. So, when he turned eighteen, the year that magical practice starts to drain your abilities, he stopped using his magic and saved it for the king. The king gave him everything he wanted. Servants, riches, slaves, and more, just to keep him from using his powers. Holding that much sorcery in for so long can make you lose your mind though. And that is what started happening to him. He became secluded in his tower, and many thought he had died. He's still there. We are all just waiting for him to show up and unleash his power on us. That's why you saving your power is so important. You are gifted, and if you have any chance against him, we need these eggs to hatch and we need them fast. Let's get back to Tarragon." Wilbur said. He led the way, as Felicity put the eggs back in her bag, two of them still glowing, ready to hatch and they hiked back to Tarragon.

The Hatchlings

FELICITY AND WILBUR made it back to Tarragon safely. Serenity was mourning the loss of her dragon Lilith. She had been wounded far too badly for Tom and Oaken to heal her. Besnik met them at the hatchling nest where Felicity was needed to hatch more eggs by magic. She had brought them the moon dragon eggs and everyone was amazed at how beautiful they were. The two that were glowing, were absolutely stunning to look at. The others were in their camouflaged state, still muddy looking but intact. They were all heavy, feeling like a ball of solid iron. She had Tom bring the other dragon egg out of the castle, to the hatchery. She knew it needed to be there anyways.

"These are so interesting!" Besnik said. He touched them gently. They were pretty amazing. Felicity couldn't deny that. Tom was holding the first dragon egg she had saved, and it was glowing now that it was closer to Felicity. At the same time, another of the moon dragon eggs was glowing brightly too.

"Look! That egg is glowing! It did that when you got close to it. That must mean that you get to have a moon dragon too. One of the most powerful dragons in the world! But then why is this one also glowing?" She said, excited that she wouldn't be the only one with a powerful beast.

"There are three out of five moon dragons that are glowing now. And this one, that you saved. Who gets the other ones?" Tom asked her.

"I don't know. I think Wilbur is going to get one though. I know he said it was rare, but two were glowing when we were in the woods. I doubt that Tristan would get one, mainly because he's gone now." She said.

"He died?" Tom asked.

"In the woods. I cut his head off. He's gone now." She told him, tears forming at the corners of her eyes.

"That's good then, isn't it? Though maybe not for you." Tom said noticing that she was still hurt by it. He knew that if she hadn't been betrayed by him, that she would have married him.

"Not exactly," Felicity replied, "Wilbur said that there was a boy that had magic, but never used it. He was locked up and forbidden to use it by Hadrion. He has all his powers and then some. When our powers are saved up like that, they unleash a deep darkness that spreads like venom. It is hard to control and dangerous should you come in contact with it. Wilbur thinks that once they find out that Tristan is gone, they will bring out this magical being and try to use them against us. We have no way of knowing or preparing for this since this is the first time in a thousand years that something like this has happened. We have to prepare now by hatching our dragons, so they train and grown. We have to use magic to make them grow faster too. It's not ideal, but we have to do it." Felicity told Tom.

Wilbur walked over to Felicity, worried and pale looking, "I have some very bad news." He told them.

"What is it?" Tom asked.

"They are bringing out the dark mage. He will be here in a week. I heard Thames talking to one of his scouts on the battlefield. He and Horace heard the men talking about it. They know Tristan is dead. There's no more time to waste. We have to get going on this. We have to hatch these moon dragons and get them trained up before something bad happens. We only have this week. They need to be hatched tonight." Wilbur looked as though he was going to be sick. He knew of the darkness all too well. He had been the best friend of the Dark Mage before he was taken by Hadrion. He knew that he was the most powerful mage of them all, especially since he was gifted already, even before he hid his powers away and had special training by the royal mage scholars. This was going to be a nasty battle that no one would win without a bit of magic.

Unexpected Warriors

THIS WAS NOW DAY FIFTEEN of the war. Felicity had hatched the moon dragons and they were growing fast, even without her magic. Wilbur hadn't been back to the dragon nest since he had made sure Felicity and the eggs had gotten there safely. She wanted him to stop by to see if one of the moon dragons was his. She had a very strong feeling that it was, even though it was rare for a dragon keeper to have more than one dragon in their lifetime. She and Tom had their dragons now though, and they loved them more than they ever thought they could. Tom's dragon, Fury, was such a cute and clumsy little thing. It was constantly tripping on its own wings and falling face first into everything.

"Come on Fury! You are supposed to be a fierce warrior not a clumsy oaf." Tom said one day, placing his hand on his forehead.

"Give him a minute. He is new to this world. You can't expect him to know how to work those wings and feet together just yet." Felicity told him.

"I know, but some of this needs to be instinct right? The other day, he landed face first in a pile of dung. He still smells bad. And your dragon is just fine. I don't know why she's all good and mine isn't. Want to trade? Mine must be defective." Tom asked.

"Never! You can't trade your destiny. And he isn't defective. You just stink at training him." Felicity laughed while Tom made a face at her. He leaned over and kissed her on the cheek, and she blushed slightly.

"I will help you train him, but ultimately, this is your dragon, and you need to learn to work together, or you will not be successful when you fight and fly." Felicity warned him.

"Yeah... ok. You're right. I will do my best then. But if he falls in poop again, I will be sending him to you." Tom half-heartedly joked. He took a whiff of his dragon again before making a face.

"Deal." Felicity said. They went back to teaching the dragons how to use their wings effectively, keep them out from underfoot, and how to use them to protect themselves and their riders when they fall, since the dragons were falling a lot anyways. After an hour of training, Wilbur finally stopped by the nest, looking for Felicity.

"Felicity, you are needed. We have a huge problem. The brought HIM!" Wilbur said. Felicity knew exactly who he meant. The dark mage. He was finally here. Just as well, it had been almost two weeks since she had killed Tristan and they knew they needed a new leader. This had to be it.

"I will be right there." She said, noticing the other hatchling that started to follow Wilbur around.

"Go away little dragon. Finish your training." Wilbur told the little one.

"She is your dragon you know." Tom told him.

"That can't be at all." Wilbur replied.

"She was glowing when you were with Felicity, she is following you now, and you don't have a dragon so you can get another one even if it is rare." Tom said.

"Shouldn't you be in the hospital with Oaken, healing the other dragons?" Wilbur snapped.

"I should be, but I have Fury and he is fine without me for now. No one has had any serious injuries yet." Tom said.

"Fine. What do you want me to do?" Wilbur asked.

"I want you to name her and see if she responds. Then we will know for sure." Tom stated.

"Fine. I guess I will call her," he paused, watching the dragon chew on a piece of fern planted near the nest, "Fern. She seems to like to eat it." Wilbur said, grumpily.

"Fern is a beautiful name. Now call her and see if she comes." Tom instructed.

"Fern. Come here, you silly dragon." Wilbur called to the small creature. She stopped chewing on the fern plant and waddled over to Wilbur, rubbing her head against his hand.

"See? She is yours." Tom said.

"That is a rare thing indeed." Wilbur was in awe. No one had ever had two dragons before. Now he did. And a moon dragon!

"Well, now you have a moon dragon to train. I think we should go check on Felicity now though. Come on, Fury." Tom said, and he and his dragon trotted off.

Wilbur looked at Fern. She was a beautiful blue creature with dark sapphire eyes. She was young but very strong looking. Felicity had been training and feeding her well. He wanted to spend more time with his dragon, but right now, they had more important things to do. The other egg hadn't hatched yet and they had to use every bit of magic left to stop this Dark Mage. They needed to have all hands-on deck and start casting more spells around the keep and the city. He turned his dragon over to another dragon trainer and rushed off towards the front lines.

Felicity and Horace were on the wall discussing the best course of action to take in order to protect the city while Thames was with Tom, trying to drag a man back behind the gate. The man was missing a leg and had passed out from blood loss and shock. Wilbur ran over to help them while Tom grabbed what he could from his bag to stop the bleeding.

"Sphagnum moss," he told Wilbur who had come over to help him and Thames, "prevents gangrene and is an antiseptic and absorbs more than a cloth. Not to mention it prevents bacteria from growing. You can use it as a water filter too, but for now, we need it for the blood. I will just pack this on there and wrap him up. We can get him to the doctor who will cauterize the wound with fire. That will be agonizing but he will live." Tom said. Wilbur was impressed that Tom had learned so much in such a short amount of time. He was always a fast learner, but this was even more impressive given the pressure he was under to heal everyone.

Thames had called for medics to come take the man away and they did. Then they all went up to where Felicity was still talking to Horace, to listen in on the plan for the Dark Mage.

"He will have powers that none of us have ever seen." Felicity told Horace.

"Yes, he will. And we have to try and get him to use up some of that power before we can truly defeat him. He needs to get weakened." Horace replied.

"I know. But how? Should we put all our energy into a shield and let him hit us as much as he can before wearing out?" Felicity asked.

"That might not be a bad idea, but we have to do this cautiously. We have magic, but so do they. Our mages aren't nearly as strong since the last war. We have to start with those who have the least amount of power first, make them think we are weak, then build back up to the stronger mage's so we can protect ourselves from his massive blows. I think he will be hitting us hard every single time though. We have to watch for that and reduce our casualties." Horace said.

"Agreed. We can do that. Draw everyone back to the keep except the front line and the mages. Have the dragon's hover over everything and blast when necessary." She replied.

"Great. I will get the word out." Horace ran off to tell the others and Wilbur stepped up to Felicity.

"I am so proud of you. You are definitely your mother's child." He told her.

Felicity smiled, "Thank you. Now if my plan works, I will be forever indebted to her and to you for taking such great care of me and teaching me everything I know." Wilbur smiled at her as an arrow sped past their heads.

Tom grabbed Felicity and Wilbur and they ducked down behind the wall. Luckily, the arrow missed whatever target it was aimed at.

"Maybe we should get off the wall now." Tom suggested.

"Great plan. Let's go spread the word to everyone and get to our own positions." Thames said, directing his men.

The Dark Mage

THIS WAS NOT YOUR AVERAGE mage. Felicity knew it. She knew that there was nothing else she could do though. She had her magic and the magic of a few others who were very much out of practice. Now that they had their dragon's, she had to find a way to make them grow faster so she could take on the Dark Mage. She had no way of properly training them to fly with a rider on their back when they are this small. She knew that if she made them grow faster, they would be physically mature enough to train, but their riders would miss out on training them and building that bond.

"I don't know what to do." She told Wilbur one day.

"What do you mean?" He asked her, wrestling a giant steak away from Fern, who was refusing to share with Fury.

"I am torn. I know that we need the extra power to fight this guy, but at the same time, I want things to happen on their own. I don't want to mess this one up. These dragons could be the last of their kind right now too. I don't want to have them die because I had to rush their training." Felicity told Wilbur.

"I know, but this isn't an option..." he paused thinking about it for a moment, "there is one thing we could try though. It will take a lot of magic and we only have a few moments to do it. They are still strategizing on their end of things, so we have only a short amount of time to make this decision. These dragons are crucial to us winning...." Wilbur was talking to himself now, pacing.

"What is it?" Felicity shouted at him, feeling impatient and anxious.

"We could use a maturity spell." He replied.

"A what?" Felicity was confused.

"A maturity spell is something that will make them both grow physically and mentally. They will get all the knowledge that you want them to have if you put it in the spell too. It is the fastest and best way to keep the dragons safe. Yes, you will miss out on them growing up," Wilbur said, noticing the look on Felicity's face, "but the world will be safe, and your dragon will live longer as an adult since their heart stays the same age." He told her.

"Ok. But what about the magic I need to fight the Dark Mage?" You don't need to worry about that. We have lots of others with magic that are practicing every day. We found many children that have magic too and even though they can't fight, we are teaching them in case they are needed. This is a fight for the world, and we are all in it together." Wilbur finished.

"I will do it then." Felicity told him.

"Then let's get started." Wilbur began to teach her. It was intricate and complicated magic. Even though she had learned a lot from her mother before she passed, she had never seen anything like this except maybe once when a dragon almost died, and her mom tried to save it. She was small and barely remembered what happened. The war had barely ended by the time she was born, and they were all living in the aftermath of it all.

Felicity waved her arms in large circles, chanted in languages she had only heard in spellcasting, and got her dragon to grow and change. She put in all the knowledge of combat, flying, and war into this tiny dragon that was now getting larger by the minute.

When she was done, Wilbur turned to her and said, "You know, you haven't named your dragon yet." Felicity thought for a moment. She wanted the name to be perfect.

"Fallon, after the Queen." Felicity said.

"I think that is the perfect name." Wilbur responded.

Felicity pet Fallon on the head. She was stretching out her new wings and testing them out. She flapped them and hovered above them for a moment before touching back down on the ground, dust settling around her.

"Fallon is the perfect name for you, my majestic one." Felicity told her, and Fallon nudged her hand. Felicity fed her half a cow as Tom came in with Fury.

"Stupid dragon! You don't eat pinecones, you eat meat. Let's get you meeeeeaaaatttt!" He said, wrestling the spiky cone away from Fury. Fury let go and Tom tumbled backwards, falling to the ground, "Damn it, Fury!" He stood up and dusted himself off.

"I can fix that problem." Felicity said, indicating to Fallon, whom Tom hadn't paid attention to since he was mad his own dragon.

"Woah! That's your dragon?" He asked her. Felicity nodded, "I can't believe you used magic to do that! Can you get my dumb dork to do that too?" He asked her.

"Only if you stop calling him names. He is a baby after all. You really need to be patient with him." She said.

"Yeah, you're right. I should be. I just can't get him to listen to me." Tom fumed.

"I know, but this is a maturity spell and if I do this, you guys need to get along." Felicity told him.

"We will. Hopefully." Tom said. Felicity rolled her eyes and got to work on Fury.

"I don't think that will happen," Wilbur whispered to Felicity, "That dragon is stubborn as a mule, and I don't think he isn't doing this on purpose just to mess with Tom." He chuckled.

Felicity smiled, "Hush now, he'll hear you. Besides, I am teaching him some mild manners, but I won't take all his mischief away from him before he's grown. That is too much fun to watch." She laughed and waved her arms around, more comfortable doing the spell for the second time around. She finished with Fury then moved to Fern. There was still one more egg and it was glowing but not hatched yet.

"Don't do anything to that dragon yet, we may not want it to hatch just yet." Wilbur said.

"What do you mean?" Felicity felt anxious again.

"Depending on its owner, who is obviously close by, we don't know if they are on our side or the side of the enemy. We must be careful."

"Agreed. Ok, we will keep it safe here and away from the enemy, just in case." Felicity replied. A loud horn blew in the distance.

"It's time to fight the Dark Mage. That was faster than I thought." Wilbur looked nervous.

"I am too tired to use magic again right now!" Felicity panicked and paced around.

"You won't have to yet. That is the last resort. We need to take the dragon's and circle around to the front lines. We have to let them see we can fight them. Let the dragon's do their job and then we will do our best to finish the rest." Wilbur said.

Felicity eyed the other dragon egg, the one she thought was hers before, the one that hasn't hatched yet. She didn't want to hatch it until she knew who it belonged to. She was scared that it would belong to someone who wouldn't care for it. The dragon knew it was around danger right now and she couldn't blame it for staying put.

As they walked through the city, smoking and destroyed, they could hear the war getting louder and louder. Screams, explosions, fires, dragon's roaring in the distance now, all of it compounded Felicity's ears and made hearing anything other than death, harder and harder. This was the final move they were about to make. This was the only way to save everyone, and Felicity knew it.

The First Strike

FELICITY DIDN'T WANT to fight. This was something she had always been against. She was a protector, not a warrior, but today, she had no choice. Tom was peaceful, too. Most of the dragon people were. Wilbur had always told her that her mother was more of a fighter than she looked, and Felicity hoped that ran true for her today. They stationed her and Fallon on the stone wall just above the gate. They considered this the best spot to attack the Dark Mage. He had nearly wiped out all the land and people before Tarragon. There was nothing but smoke, ash, and bodies between the stumps of the trees. He had unleashed so much chaos that there was nothing more for Felicity to save, albeit the people behind the gates.

She could see the Mage on his own Night Mare, watching her with a bit of curiosity. He seemed eager to use more magic against her and the rest of the people of the Northern City. She felt as though she had seen him before but could not place it. The family that she had heard of, the one that mistreated him, she wondered who that was. Who brought him to the King?

"Please, just leave us alone! We want no more violence." Thames called out, "We just want the dragons to be free and live in peace with their owners. No one needs to be hurt anymore."

"If you give us the dragons you have, you can go free. Until then, we will continue to fight you." The Mage shouted in a deep, booming voice. Clearly, he was now running the show.

Felicity felt some sort of strange connection to this Mage. She didn't know why. Felicity felt the need to ask Wilbur, who was standing next to her with Fern, "Why do I know him?" She asked.

"I was hoping you wouldn't, but I guess it was unavoidable. That is Marco, your brother." Wilbur saw the shock on Felicity's face. He knew this would be hard for her to comprehend, so he continued, "Your mother was married to another man for a while. He was cruel to her and your older brother, and she often went out to escape his wrath. She met your father and became pregnant with you. The man found out that the baby wasn't his, so he abandoned him with another family. They also abused him. But one day, the King met him on the road when your brother had stolen a dragon's egg. The King found out about his powers. He could heal dragons, he could train them and make them grow, and he could create life within a dragon if he needed to, even though no one can make a dragon give birth. Marco was the ultimate Keeper of the dragons, the way you were, but he wanted more from him. They locked him up and told him to never use his magic so they could use it for gain later. A war. It was also a punishment for your mother since she had to see her son taken away from her and locked in a cage by someone as toxic and horrid as Hadrion. It's why he wanted you to hatch the dragons and use your magic so your brother could be his ultimate warrior. Your mother never stopped trying to save him, though. That was part of her plan the night she was caught and killed. She saved the dragon egg you possess, but was caught and slaughtered when she went back for more eggs and your brother and you. The rumor is that the egg you have in your possession, the one in the nursery, belongs to him. She saved the egg first because she knew that was what he would have wanted. Why it has been shaking and glowing, I don't know. He isn't near it enough to be sensed. Or maybe he is? It could be part of his more powerful gift. Marco had always wanted to be a Dragon Keeper. He has transformed into a monster and been torn apart inside, so much so that he can only feel anger and hate and that is dangerous for anyone with dragon magic to feel. If he had a dragon now, we would all be finished.

Felicity took a breath. She had a brother. Not just any brother, but one she had to destroy before he took the lives of everyone she loved. What was worse was that she had his dragon. What would happen if she killed her brother before the dragon hatched? She had no idea what to do now except fight.

Brotherly Love

THE DARK MAGE AND FELICITY stared each other down as both sides tried to figure out what to do next. They knew that this would be a battle of magic now. Felicity had used her powers some, but not to the extent that others had. There was only so much magic left in Tarragon, and Marco had most of the magic outside the wall. She looked to Thames, Wilbur, and Tom who were standing with her on the wall, dragons for each of them except for Thames, who let his dragon sit with Serenity as a comfort.

"I want to talk to Marco." Felicity told them.

"What?" Tom asked.

"He's... my brother. I don't think he knows that. I want to talk to him. See if I can reason with him first. I don't want to hurt him, and I definitely don't want to kill him. I just want to make sure he knows who I am and that I have his dragon." Felicity said, quietly.

"This is a bad idea," Wilbur told her, "But I think it could be worth a shot. I will have to go with you, and I want to bring Besnik with us. He was there in the prison at one point, with Marco." Wilbur said.

"Fine. I can agree with that. Let's bring out the temporary flag of peace and go to them." Felicity replied.

They got Besnik, who was down by the gate, clutching a stitch in his side, leaning against the stone wall. He was dirty and scraped up, but otherwise unharmed. Besnik had his own moon dragon too, but he opted to leave his young and so he was left behind the wall.

"We need your help. I want to talk to Marco." Felicity told him.

"Are you crazy? We can't just go up to him and have a friendly chat. He is vicious and angry. He will kill us all if we even go near him." Besnik told her.

"He won't if he finds out he's my brother and I have his dragon egg." Felicity told him.

Besnik's mouth dropped open. "You're the one he wants to see then." Besnik said.

"What do you mean?" Wilbur asked.

He was not far away from me when I was temporarily locked up in the prison thanks to Tristan. I could hear him screaming into the night over the bad dreams and the torment that they had placed upon him. One night, I was able to get close enough to his cell that I could roll a biscuit to him through the bars without being seen. He had just been punished for trying to use his magic, so they were starving him for three days. I couldn't hear him very well, but he told me that a few years after they locked him up, one of his guards told him that his mother was about to have another baby. Then when you were born, he was told that it was a sister. He didn't know your name or anything. Marco said he felt both happy and angry with you. He wanted your freedom and your love at the same time. If you really are his sister, then this might be a dangerous game to play. But I think that if you are ready for it, then we must go now while the dead are being taken care of." He stood back up, used his sword as a cane, and started limping towards the gate.

"Let's go then." Wilbur said. Fern and Fallon followed behind them.

They walked out of the gates and made their way towards the Dark Mage. He was still on top of his Night Mare, which was spooked when the dragons approached. Felicity told their beasts to stay back and marched directly up to Marco.

"I am your sister, and I am sorry about the life you had to live. I never wanted that for you, nor did I know of your existence, or I would have saved you." She patted the Night Mare on the snout and looked at Marco in the eyes. He looked as though he was going to cry at first, then dismounted.

"Hello sister. At least we finally got to meet. Too bad I still have to kill you." He snarled.

"Did I mention that I have your dragon?" She added. He looked shocked, then calmed himself.

"No, is that her?" He pointed to Fallon.

"No. I have a dragon too. Yours hasn't hatched yet and it never will, unless you surrender to us. There is no ruler in Domandun now. Tristan and Hadrion are both dead and you and the rest of the Mage's are free to live in your city or wherever you want. I know that you have hate in you. I would too. But this isn't the way to do things, and I can see why the moon dragons don't want anything to do with you. Most Keeper's get one. You won't even get your basic dragon if you don't change your ways. They won't go to anyone evil." Felicity said.

"You will never survive me, little sister. I am far too powerful for you." He powered up a spell in his hands and blasted her off her feet. "I will have my dragon and there is nothing you can do about it."

Felicity stood up, and she and Besnik mounted Fallon while Wilbur got on Fern's back, and they retreated towards the gate.

Dragon Heist

FELICITY LANDED FALLON just behind the gate and dismounted. Thames rushed up to her to make sure she was ok. Besnik and Wilber were talking viciously in off to the side about Marco while Tom and Oaken were checking on the dragons to make sure they were fed and watered.

"I can't believe Marco wants to be at war. I get that he's mad, but this is insane! Doesn't he see that people are dying? They will eventually run out of magic and people and then what?" Felicity was pacing, furious as ever.

"Look, we have done all we can to stop this war. Now we need to wear him down." Thames said.

"What do you mean?" Felicity asked, kicking a rock.

"We need to get him to use his powers up and weaken himself. He has already used about a year's worth of spells, but now we need him to use more. This is the only way to get him to be defeated. We have magic here but not enough put together to stand up to him. We need decoys." Thames replied.

"How do we do that?" Felicity questioned.

"We wait for nightfall and use our practice dummies to distract him. We place them all over the wall, then he will attack them, and will use up more power but with us loosing less people. Then we bring out the dragons to blaze them all and then hit them with potions and spells." Thames replied.

"Potions?" Felicity never practiced potion craft and had no idea what that would do.

"Yes, I may have had a few of our mage's working on potions that would do some damage to these guys. Mainly things like making them sick or giving them hallucinations that would terrify them into insanity. Nothing big." Thames said with a smile.

"Brilliant choice! I can't wait to see this go down." Besnik said, nudging Tom who was feeding Fallon a dead chicken.

"I suppose we have no choice. They wanted this fight so a fight they will get." Felicity adjusted her armor and looked at the rest of the group. She was not a fighter, but she knew that in order to protect everyone, she had to be. This was the only way to do it. She rubbed Fallon on her hard, smooth snout and took a breath. "Let's spread the word and get this plan in motion. We need the second battalion back in to give the first battalion a break, get the third battalion ready to execute the plan. Let's keep cycling our warriors in and out. I also have a feeling that Marco will try and get his dragon tonight. We need to put extra security on that. I don't want him to even see the egg, let alone get it. If he does, then we really will have no chance of survival at all." Thames looked at Felicity and saw the fierceness in her as she spoke.

"Ok then, let's get to work." Thames set off to ready the different battalion's that they had new duties to complete. Wilbur and Besnik went to sharpen their swords as they planned to guard Marco's dragon egg, and Tom and Oaken were adjusting the armor on the dragons to get them ready for war. Felicity went to rest in a nearby tent. There was hardly any time left for them to rest now that the battle was going to hit a peak. She tried to sleep but her mind was busy and the rest she had was not good. At least her body was ready to get up again even if her mind told her that she needed another six hours. She got up and went out at twilight to see the soldier's swapping places and Thames guiding his men as to what to do with the dummies that were to go on the wall. They had put them in armor and gave them bows and swords. This was the plan that they had to complete. This was the one thing that had to work. Felicity needed to kill Marco.

Finish This

NIGHT FELL AND THE decoys were all set up. Felicity and Thames were standing behind the wall with Fallon, ready to mount her and take flight the second they were summoned to.

"Are you sure this plan will work?" Felicity asked Thames, a bit nervously even though this was both their plans.

"Yes, I am almost positive this won't fail." He laughed nervously, trying to cut the tension.

Felicity smiled, "Ok but jokes aside, do you think that this will work out for us?" She was terrified. She had no idea what would happen after this battle. It had been a month of fighting already.

"I really can't say. All I know is that we need to kill Marco and many of the other mage's are losing their powers now too. He is still the most powerful one in this situation and we are not able to hold off for much longer, but we are getting closer to victory and further from a sudden death as we go. We have to try, right?" Thames had a way of reassuring her.

"Indeed, we do." Serenity said, walking up to Thames with Lilith behind her.

"You're both ok!" Felicity shouted, flinging her arms around them.

"Yeah, it was a close call though. We can't take too many chances now, but I am willing to fight side by side with you." She said. "I just can't have her out there. She nearly died. She can't fly anymore, and I am sorry we won't be that much help."

"I will take all the help I can get." Felicity said, noticing Lilith had lost part of her right wing.

"Good. Because here we go..." Thames said. He triggered the decoys, and the blasting started. They could hear Marco shooting off spells along with the mage's that still had magic left. Tom, Wilbur, and Besnik were stationed behind several of the decoys, letting out screams of agony, giving more realness to the fake men that were being blown up.

"Damn it!" Wilbur shouted really loudly after Marco through a fireball at him.

Thames and Felicity rushed to his side, "What happened?" Thames asked.

"I got burned." Wilbur showed them his leg that had melted fabric sticking to it.

"Tom!" Felicity shouted, bringing him to her side, "Can you heal him?" She asked, desperately.

"I can spare a bit of medicine and magic for that." He took a large leaf of aloe out of his bag, sliced it open and placed it on Wilbur's leg, gel side down. He wrapped Wilbur's leg up with a scrap of fabric, muttered some spell under his breath, then unwrapped Wilbur's leg. There was now a shiny, pink patch where the burn had been, and part of his pants were gone up to the knee, but he was fine.

Wilbur flexed his leg, "Doesn't hurt. That's going to be a cool scar when it finishes healing." He laughed. Everyone went back to their posts, dodging fireballs and lightning strikes as Marco and his men advanced. Besnik rushed down the wall and raced to Felicity.

"It's time to unleash the dragon fire." He said, amused with himself. Felicity and Thames mounted Fallon, followed by Serenity and Lilith. They flew high over the dark land with the exception of Lilith who climbed and perched on the top of the gate, taking in the death of both people and land. It made Felicity want to cry seeing all the ruins from the sky. Fallon, Lilith, and several other dragons that had been entrusted with the task of blowing out a blanket of fire across the battlefield.

Felicity felt Fallon's body grow hot as she puffed her flame out on an already destroyed land. The heat from the other dragons in this ring of fire move was intense. Marco tried to counter their flames with ice, but there were too many of them. The fell back and fled into the woods. Marco was too weak now to destroy anything. It was over, for now.

Rebuilding

EVERYONE WAS EXHAUSTED. Battle had taken its toll on everyone. Felicity still requested that they keep soldiers on the gate overnight and that those who were able to go out and collect the bodies of those who were out there. They were planning to burry every single person and they had brought the women and children out hiding, so they could help dress the bodies of their loved ones and bury them. It was not an easy task and there was wailing and tears from everyone. This was the time to start rebuilding the city though. Felicity couldn't help but think about what would happen in Domandun. She considered trying to unite their cities but had to wait and see what the people there would do if they saw her again. She no longer looked like her old self when she was Andromeda, and she had completely created a new life as Felicity. She wasn't against magic, but she was against those who were part of Tristan's gang and knew that their families would be angry once they discovered that their loved ones were not coming back thanks to her plan.

Marco's body was confirmed found by Wilbur who had gone out to help the men load people into wagons. Though Felicity didn't remember him being killed by the fire. She saw some men that had perished, but not him.

"I am sorry about your loss. I know you wanted to fix him and have a family. He was just too angry and unable to control himself." Wilbur told her as she sobbed. It was hard to kill family, even if they were horrible and dangerous.

"I know it's for the best, but I don't really like it." Felicity told him.

"I know. It's going to be ok though. We can rebuild the world again and you kept the dragon's safe. They won't be poached anymore. At least not by the Mage's." He said.

"That's the best news I think I've heard since the start of the war." Felicity went back to the castle, which fortunately, was still standing unscathed. She wished Queen Fallon had survived long enough to see this end. For the next few weeks, they mourned the dead and buried them. Then they moved on to rebuilding the homes that were destroyed, then the wall. It took months for everything to start looking as it did before. Felicity made a note to build more improvements on their wall and give them more security just in case something like this was to happen again. She still couldn't shake the feeling that something was off about Marco. She didn't think he had died.

Felicity knew she should rest, but she struggled to. She had a kingdom to rule with Tom, Thames, Wilbur, and Besnik by her side. She made Thames and Wilbur her official advisors who also oversaw her army. Besnik and Tom were sent to care for and protect the dragons, Marco's egg was still glowing, and she wondered if it was really his to begin with. Tom became a very skilled healer for both people and dragons. Oaken stayed in his position as dragon healer and kept training others to heal dragons and people, even those without magic.

In the end, Felicity and Tom were able to get married about a year after the war had ended. This was no surprise to anyone. They had been waiting for this to happen. Tom became the King but allowed Felicity to focus on the royal things while he played with dragons all day. One spring morning, Felicity had met with Oaken and the midwife. She suspected something was stirring within her and had it confirmed before going down to the nest of dragons.

"Tom, I have something to tell you." She said to him, as he walked out of the nest.

"Me too. But you go first." He told her.

"I'm pregnant." She told him. He got excited and hugged and kissed her. "What was your news?" Felicity asked him.

"Marco's egg, it's starting to hatch." He said. They both looked at the egg.

"Does this mean it belongs to our child or is Marco still alive?" Felicity asked Tom.

"They said they found his body out in the field. Or at least what was left of it. Everyone was burnt to a crisp." Tom replied.

"I know. That's what worries me. He has magic the same as I do. He could easily have tricked us somehow. Who does this last egg belong to and who will get the other two moon dragons?" Felicity questioned.

"I don't know. But our child hasn't been born yet, nor have you been near the other moon dragons since carrying our child. These dragons could belong to anyone." Tom told her. Just then, one of the moon dragons came up to Felicity and sniffed her stomach. It began to bounce around and get excited.

"I think we know who will get this dragon then." Felicity said.

"Agreed. Our child will have their dragon before they are old enough to walk." Tom chuckled. "But then, that leaves two more." The other moon dragon was flying around and not paying any attention to them, too busy playing with Fury to care, while Marco's egg continued to glow. The new age of Dragon Keepers was about to be born.

Don't miss out!

Visit the website below and you can sign up to receive emails whenever Abby Woodland publishes a new book. There's no charge and no obligation.

https://books2read.com/r/B-A-JGXZ-ZNEOC

BOOKS 2 READ

Connecting independent readers to independent writers.

Did you love *The Dragon Keeper*? Then you should read *The Raze*[1] by Abby Woodland!

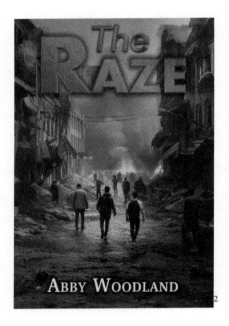

[2]

The government has taken control. There is no escape. You either join in or die trying.

Read more at www.abbywoodland.com.

Also by Abby Woodland

The Raze
The Dragon Keeper

Watch for more at www.abbywoodland.com.

About the Author

Abby Woodland lives in Arizona with her daughter and large extended family. She is a musician, prepper, Kindle Vella author, and complete book nerd. If she's not writing, she's editing, playing guitar, going on walks, or advocating for mental health and those with special needs.

Read more at www.abbywoodland.com.

Milton Keynes UK
Ingram Content Group UK Ltd.
UKHW041049290923
429627UK00001B/16

9 798223 599944